BRAM STOKER'S

DRACULA

FOR KIDS

CLASSICS FOR KIDS

BRAM STOKER'S

DRACULA

FOR KIDS

by
Luke Hayes

J. Porter Publishing

J. Porter Publishing
JporterPublishing.com

Classics For Kids: Dracula for Kids
ISBN: 978-0-9831484-1-8

Printed in the United States of America on acid-free paper
Design: Joy Taylor

BRAM STOKER'S

DRACULA

FOR KIDS

Chapter 1

I had not slept well. Strange dreams troubled me during the night. A dog kept howling. The food in Transylvania did not agree with me. Paprika on everything.

In the morning, while I was eating breakfast, the landlady of the old hotel where I was staying approached me.

"You are Herr Harker? Jonathan Harker?"

"Yes, that's me."

"I have letter for you."

I opened it and read,

> *My Friend,*
> *Welcome to Transylvania. Tomorrow take the stagecoach to the*
> *Borgo Pass. My carriage will meet you there and bring you to me.*
> *Most sincerely,*
>
> *DRACULA*

Good. My journey was finally over. I had traveled all across Europe, starting in England weeks ago. I had journeyed over mountains and up long rivers. Transylvania had to be one of the wildest parts of the continent. None of my maps was up to date. Certainly none showed the castle of the person I had come to see, Count Dracula.

I was anxious to meeting the Count. Maybe he could explain all the weird things I had seen along the way, things I was still seeing.

The ancestors of the folks in this region were Huns and Turks, wild people. The men here wore their hair long. Each had a thick black mustache and dark eyes. They looked at me with suspicion.

I keep hearing strange noises at night. I see eyes staring at me from the darkness of the woods as I pass by on the road.

I have been noting everything in this journal so that I can tell Mina all about it when I get home. She and I are going to be married next year. She's always curious about my work.

I am a lawyer. Count Dracula wrote to my firm in London about a house he had purchased there. He asked me to come out here to his home to help him make the deal final.

"Do you know Count Dracula?" I asked the hotel landlady when I arrived.

She looked at me and quickly crossed herself. "Never heard of this man," she said.

"I must contact him. I was told he lives in this region."

"I know nothing. Do not ask more about him. Bad luck."

"Why is that? Is he dishonest?"

She shook her head and turned away. Yet now she was bringing me the message from him. How strange.

It was even more disturbing when she said, "Do not go to him, young gentleman. By no means. You must not go!"

"Why? Why shouldn't I visit him?"

"Tonight is feast of St. George. When midnight come, all evil things gain power. Do not you know where you go? Do not you know what can happen?"

"I know I'm going to see a man about business," I said. "That's all. I've come a long way and I don't see any reason to turn back now. As for the other, we don't believe in superstitions in England. We're more advanced than that."

"Please," the woman pleaded. She dropped to her knees and begged me not to go. "For your mother's sake. Do not! Do not go!"

When the stagecoach stopped to pick me up, the landlady spoke with the driver. I don't speak the language very well, but I heard them say words that I know meant *devils* and *evil spirits* and *danger*.

I'll have to remember to ask Count Dracula about all these silly local beliefs, I thought to myself. He'll be able to explain them.

Before I could climb into the coach, the landlady placed a cross around my neck. She also handed me a head of garlic and told me to carry it in my pocket.

"May heaven bless and protect you, young man."

The coach carried me and some other passengers out into the countryside. I tossed the garlic out so that the smell wouldn't offend my fellow travelers. Silly superstition!

I watched out the window at the dark, wild pine woods. The driver had to whip the horses to get them to pull us up the steep hills. The rough road made the coach rock back and forth violently. Finally it stopped in a remote and desolate spot.

"This is Borgo Pass, Herr Harker," the driver yelled to me.

I climbed out and looked around. It was a gap between two mountains. The wind moaned through the trees. Fog hung in the branches. The air felt icy.

There was no carriage waiting. No one was around. It was the most desolate place I had ever seen.

"Can you wait until Count Dracula's carriage arrives? I don't want to be left alone in the middle of nowhere."

"Can't wait," the driver said. "Other passengers must go on. Not good, this place. You should not stay here. Danger!"

Just then a carriage appeared, drawn by four black horses and driven by a tall man in a large black hat. His face was hidden in shadow.

"Stop trying to scare this good gentleman," the driver said to the coachman. "Give me his baggage, you fool."

The tall driver held out a hand to help me into the carriage. His grip was like steel. From working with horses, I guessed. His eyes peered at me from dark slits. He gave me a thin smile, and I noticed that his teeth were very white, and very sharp.

The stagecoach and its passengers continued on, leaving me alone with the carriage and this mysterious driver. A cold wind tumbled down the mountain, making me shiver.

"The nights are cold here," the driver said. "My master, the Count, asked that I take good care of you. I have brought a rug to keep you warm. Under the seat you will find a bottle of plum brandy. Relax and enjoy the ride."

I tried to relax, but this country was too strange. We seemed to be going in circles through the night. I called out to the driver, asking him how far it was to the count's castle.

"Not far," was all he said.

I struck a match and looked at my watch. I saw that it was nearly midnight. I tried a sip of the plum brandy, but it did not warm me.

Somewhere in the distance a dog howled. Farther off, another answered. A minute later another, sharper howl echoed through the mountains. I could tell that this was not a dog but a wolf. The horses stopped. They reared up. The driver whipped them. They plunged ahead. I was growing more fearful by the minute.

The carriage continued on into the night. It passed through a tunnel of dark trees. The wind wailed and grew very cold. Snow began to fall. Now, on every side, I heard the howling of the wolves. Closer and closer. The driver didn't seem worried by them.

Now the driver stopped the carriage. He jumped down and ran off toward mysterious blue flames that burned in the woods. I wasn't sure, but I thought I could see the flame shining right through the body of the driver. It was as if he were made of glass.

I waited nervously for him to return. Then the horses started to tremble and whinny with fright.

What could the matter be? I didn't hear any wolves howling now.

I peered out into the darkness. I could see nothing but dark forest. No, wait — I saw creatures. Yes, they were wolves. And they were surrounding the carriage. There must have been fifty of them. They were eerily quiet. They just stared at me. Their silence was worse than their howling. All alone in the dark, I was so terrified that I couldn't move.

Suddenly the moon burst from behind a cloud. Now I could see their slick white teeth and red tongues and shaggy hair. They all began to howl at once. The horses jumped and reared and rolled their eyes. I beat on the side of the carriage to scare the terrible beasts away.

The wolves just came closer.

Chapter 2

I was trapped in a carriage in the dark with vicious wolves all around. Will this be the end of me? I wondered.

Just as the wolves were closing in on the carriage, I heard the driver returning. They'll attack him and tear him to pieces, I thought.

But he just waved his arm and ordered the wolves back. Strangely, they obeyed his command. It was as if they understood him. They slunk back away from the carriage.

What a strange incident! The driver mounted the carriage without a word. He whipped the horses to get them going. I shook with fear as we continued into the mountains. On and on we went, ever upward.

I must have fallen asleep. Maybe there was a sleeping potion in that plum brandy. The next thing I knew, we were stopped in a courtyard before a huge stone castle. I again felt the driver's icy grip as he helped me down from the carriage. He led the horses through an archway and was gone. I stood there alone in the dark.

Was this a dream? A nightmare? What kind of strange adventure had I gotten into? There was no knocker on the door. I began to feel trapped.

Then chains rattled and I heard a loud squeeee-ak. The heavy door swung back. A tall man, dressed all in black, looked out at me.

"Welcome to the house of Dracula, dear sir," he said. "Enter of your own will. Of your own will, mind you!"

What did he mean? I stepped inside and the man grasped my hand. His own hand was cold as ice. It felt like the hand of a dead man, but his grip was terribly strong, like iron. It reminded me of the hand of that carriage driver.

"Are you Count Dracula?" I asked.

"I am Dracula. You are very welcome here, Mr. Harker."

The Count carried my bags himself. Odd, I thought. He must have servants. Where are they? He took me to a room with a fireplace. The warmth of the fire felt good.

"Your supper will be ready as soon as you've had a chance to refresh yourself," he said. "It is a hard journey, I know."

A few minutes later, I sat down to a tasty roast chicken with turnips. The Count said that he would not join me, he had already eaten. He asked me many questions about my trip. How did I like his country? Had I been treated well in town? Had any of the peasants been telling me stories?

I said they had mentioned something about the feast of St. George and evil spirits.

"They have many strange superstitions," he said. "They talk too much."

During the supper, I had a chance to get a good look at the Count. He was quite an old man, with a high forehead. His thick eyebrows nearly met over his nose. Below his white mustache his teeth stuck out over his thin red lips. They were unusually sharp looking. His ears were pointed. His skin was very pale, whiter than I had seen on any man.

The Count's hands were truly bizarre. They were as thick as the paws of an animal and hair grew from his palms. His fingernails were long and pointed, like claws. When he reached out to touch me, it made me feel a little sick.

I didn't realize how late it was until I looked out the window. In the east I could see the first light of dawn. Everything was very still. From the valley below, I heard the sound of wolves howling. Many wolves.

The Count looked at me with gleaming eyes. He said, "Listen to them. They are the children of the night. What music they make!"

What music, indeed.

He bid me good night and left me alone. It had certainly been the strangest day of my life.

Tired from my long journey, I didn't awake until afternoon. Breakfast was waiting for me in my room. A note from the Count said he could not meet with me until later.

After I ate, I wandered around the castle. Everything seemed very luxurious. The plates were pure gold. They had to be valuable antiques. Everything there was very old. I wanted to comb my hair, but I could not find a mirror. Not in the bathroom, not anywhere. And I still saw no servants. Who took care of this big castle? It was one of the loneliest places I had ever been.

I spent some time in the Count's library. He had many books about England, as well as maps of London and other cities. But most of the volumes were in a language I didn't know. They looked very old.

As evening was coming on, the Count joined me.

"I have read everything I could about your country," he said. "I hope you can teach me to speak your language."

"But you speak English perfectly," I answered.

"No, I don't. Anyone in London who heard me would consider me a stranger. When I move there, I want to seem like everyone else. I want to fit in."

"I see," I said. "Your plan is to settle in England?"

"That's right. As you know, different countries have different customs. Here in Transylvania, our ways are not your ways. You may find things to be rather strange here. In fact, you've already told me about the strange events on your trip."

"Yes, it was rather difficult."

"But let's get down to business," he said. "Tell me all about my new house in London."

"The estate is called Carfax," I said. I showed him the papers that related to the purchase. "It's a very old house, one of the oldest in that area. Nearby is a deep pond. Also, an abandoned chapel. There are only a few other houses nearby. I should mention that one of them has been turned into a private lunatic asylum. You can't see it from your house, but some might find it disturbing."

"I am very happy that the house is old," he said. "I could not live in a new house. The chapel is good, too. That means there's a graveyard. Gloomy places delight me. I wish to be alone with my thoughts. And a lunatic asylum means nothing to me. I am not afraid of crazy people. I like them."

Again the Count did not join me at supper, saying he wasn't hungry. After I ate, we talked for many hours. When the first rooster crowed to announce the dawn, the Count leaped to his feet.

"Your descriptions of England are too interesting," the Count said. "I forget how time flies. I must let you get to bed."

I slept for a few hours. When I awoke, I started to shave myself, using a small mirror I had brought with me. Without warning, I felt a hand on my shoulder. Startled, I spun around. Dracula was staring at me.

"Good morning," the Count said.

What amazed me was that I had not seen the Count approach. I looked into the mirror again. It was true! The Count stood in front of the glass, yet his image did not appear there.

I had cut myself while shaving. The Count stared at the trickle of blood that ran down my neck. His eyes blazed with fury. He grabbed for my throat. Then he spotted the cross that the old woman at the hotel had hung around my neck. He immediately shrank back.

"You should be careful not to cut yourself in this country," Dracula said quite calmly. "It is very dangerous. And you won't need this. Away with it!" He took my mirror and flung it out the window. I could hear it shatter outside on the rocks.

What kind of behavior was this? For some reason, I didn't feel I was able to object. I felt weak and afraid.

Again I ate breakfast alone. I had yet to see the Count eat or drink a thing. What did he live on? Surely, this was a strange man.

When I finished, I explored the castle. I found that the building stood on the edge of a steep cliff. On three sides, anything thrown from a window would fall a thousand feet. Beyond, I could see nothing but empty woods.

I soon discovered something else. All the doors leading to the outside were locked. Was the castle a prison? Was I a prisoner?

When I returned to my room, I found the Count making my bed. So it was true! I had suspected that the count had no servants in his castle. There was no one here to wait on him.

That meant I was alone with Dracula. I saw now that Dracula must have been the driver of the carriage. He had been the one who had controlled the wild wolves.

I knew now that I was in some kind of danger. I was glad that the old lady had made me wear the cross. That seemed to have the power to protect me.

I wanted to get the Count to talk more about himself. Maybe I could uncover something of his mystery. I knew that I had to be very careful. I did not want to arouse the Count's suspicion. I sensed danger around him.

That night, during our long talk over dinner, Dracula spoke of ancient history as if it had happened only yesterday. He talked about long-ago wars as if he had fought in them himself. His people had repelled foreign invaders, he said. They had won great and bloody battles.

"But those warlike days are gone," he said. "Blood is too precious today. Far too precious to shed in senseless combat."

The dawn was just breaking. The Count hurried off to bed, as he did every night.

I spent the day again studying books in his library. In the evening, I talked over legal matters with the Count. After all, that was why I had come here.

"I may wish to ship some valuable goods to a port in England," he said. "I would need a lawyer to claim them."

"We could arrange that with a good firm that I know and trust," I suggested.

"Can't a man in England have two lawyers?" he asked.

"Of course," I said. "Men of business who do not like to have any one person know all of their affairs will often hire another lawyer."

"That's good!" the Count said. "Now I would like you to write to your employer and to your friends to let them know you are staying with me for a month."

My heart grew cold at his words. "So long?" I asked. "I don't think—"

"I will accept no refusal," the Count said.

What could I do but agree? My employer, Mr. Hawkins, had told me to do whatever I could for the Count. He was a valuable client.

"Don't mention anything in your letters except business," the Count warned. "Tell them you are well and looking forward to seeing them, that's all."

Dracula smiled as he handed me the writing paper. I noticed the Count's two sharp teeth pressed over his lower lip.

Before he left me alone, the Count mentioned that he would be busy tonight and that we would not be able to have our usual talk.

"I must warn you," he said, "that you should not sleep anywhere in the castle except in your own room. There are many memories here, ancient vapors. They may bring on nightmares. If you feel yourself getting sleepy, always hurry back to your room. There you will be safe."

I wondered if the nightmares he was talking about could be any worse than the one I was living at that very moment. That night I left my room and went to a staircase window where I could look out. The scene below was bathed in soft yellow moonlight. The valleys were utterly black.

For a long time, I gazed on this eerie landscape Then I saw a sudden movement. It came from the window of the Count's own room. I ducked my head in so that I couldn't be seen.

When I looked again, I saw the Count's head coming out his window. I could not see his face, but I could not mistake those powerful hands with the hairy palms.

I was amazed. The Count slowly came out of the window and began to crawl down the castle wall headfirst. His black cloak was spread out like wings. I could not believe my eyes. No man could perform such a feat.

It must be a trick of the moonlight, I thought. Some weird effect of shadow.

But I could not deny what I saw. Dracula was clinging to the cracks in the stones. He was climbing down the wall like a giant black lizard!

Chapter 3

I now knew that I must escape. I was afraid that if I did not leave this awful place I would die here. Knowing that Dracula was out, I crept through the castle again. I tried every door. Each was locked. The Count must keep the keys with him. My only hope was to get into Dracula's room and steal those keys.

At last, I found a door that was not locked. As I pushed on it, it swung back on rusty hinges, making a loud creaking sound. Beyond was another wing of the castle. I knew I might not have this chance to explore again. I tiptoed ahead into the darkness.

It appeared that ladies must have once lived in this part of the castle. The furniture looked more elegant and more comfortable. All was covered with thick dust, but I saw some patches of color in the moonlight. The rest of the castle was drab.

I trembled with fear. Even so, I was glad to get away from the Count. I sat down on a couch and looked out the window. The moonlit night was quite lovely. I felt tired, but I remembered the Count's warning. Do not sleep in any but my own room. Why?

I won't obey him, I thought. Why shouldn't I sleep wherever I like? What could possibly happen?

I felt more and more sleepy as I sat there. I began to drowse off. As in a dream, three women appeared and were standing around me. They were watching me closely. I heard them whisper together. Two were dark-haired. They had the same red piercing eyes as the Count. The third had golden hair and gleaming green eyes. All their lips were as red as rubies. Their teeth were brilliant white and had sharp points.

The two dark women chuckled. They said to the fair one, "You go first. We will follow. He is young and strong. There are enough kisses for all of us."

To me, it seemed just like a dream. I tried to stand but I could not move.

The golden-haired woman came and bent over me. I could feel her breath on my neck. Most people's breath is warm, hers was cold. It smelled sweet. But it also had a sharper aroma. Like the smell of blood.

She knelt beside me. Through my half-open eyes, I saw her lick her lips like an animal. Her tongue moved over her sharp white teeth. The skin of my throat tickled as she came nearer and nearer. Then two of her sharp teeth touched me.

Suddenly she drew back with a start.

The count came striding across the room. He grabbed the slender neck of the fair-haired woman. He glared at her, furious. He bared his teeth in rage. He hurled the woman across the room. The others drew backward.

"You dare to touch him?" he cried. "After what I told you? This man belongs to me!"

The women shrunk back, afraid. But they also laughed. They laughed a laugh so cold that it made me shiver to hear it.

"When I am finished with him," the Count said, "kiss him all you want. But until then you must not touch him. If you three are so hungry, satisfy yourselves with this."

He tossed a bag onto the floor. It moved as if it contained something alive. One of the women rushed to open it. I heard a cry. It sounded like the wail of a baby. The others gathered round. Then they all faded into the moonlight.

I awoke in my own bed. I must have been here all along, I thought.

What an awful, crazy nightmare. Thankfully, it was just a dream. It was over.

Or was it? Did three women live in this castle? Were they waiting to fall on me while I slept? Waiting to "kiss" me on the neck? No, it couldn't be.

That night the Count asked me to write more letters back home.

"The first will say that your work is nearly done. Next, you will write that you are starting for home soon. The third will say that you have left the castle and are on your way."

I had no choice. I had to go along with his plan. He told me to date the letters June 12, June 19 and June 29. So now I knew exactly how long I had to live. The next few weeks would decide my fate.

I must get word out, I thought. The day before, I had seen a group of gypsies passing by outside the castle. Maybe I could get them to mail letters for me. That way I could contact my friends in England before... before what?

I will write to Mina in shorthand code, I thought. No one will be able to read it but her. I will write to Mr. Hawkins, my employer. I will tell him to expect news from her.

I wrote the letters. When I saw the gypsies passing, I threw the packet down to them. I also tossed them a gold piece. They took the letters and bowed, as if they understood. But did they? Would they mail them? Or would they take the money and throw the letters away?

I soon found out they did neither. The next day the Count appeared in my room.

"The gypsies have given me two letters," he said. "One is from you to Mr. Hawkins. That's fine, I will see that it is sent along. The other contains strange symbols. I'm afraid it's some kind of magic spell that could bring you bad luck. I am afraid I must destroy it."

With that, he threw my letter to Mina into the fire. Afterward, I found that my all the paper and envelopes in the castle had disappeared. Now there was no hope that I would be saved.

The next day some deliverymen came to the castle. I ran to my window.

"Help me!" I shouted. "Please help me!"

I suppose they did not understand English. They looked at me as if I were a madman. One of them said something and the others laughed. I watched them unload a shipment of large wooden boxes. A whole large pile of boxes, maybe fifty or sixty of them. Each one had a rope handle.

That night, I again watched Dracula crawl down the side of the castle. This time I was shocked to find that the Count was wearing one of my own suits. And he was carrying the same bag I had seen him throw to the three women.

Later, I heard him return. Just at that moment, a wail came from the courtyard of the castle. I saw a woman standing outside. When she saw me at the window, she screamed. I could understand a few of the words.

"Monster!" she was saying. "Give me my child!"

She ran to the huge door and beat against it with her fists. From another window, I heard the Count's voice.

A pack of wolves appeared in the courtyard. The woman hardly had time to scream in fear before they were on her. There was a brief struggle. Then the wolves went away, licking their lips.

The next day, I figured it was now or never. I made my most desperate effort yet to escape. Removing my boots, I climbed out onto the narrow stone ledge that ran across the castle wall. I didn't dare look down. I edged along until I reached the Count's room. I was determined to find those keys.

There was no one in the room. I looked all over but could not find any keys. I did uncover a pile of gold. There were coins from countries around the world. I found a small door and opened it. It down a stone passageway. It passed like a tunnel into the ruins of a chapel. The smell was sickly and disgusting.

There inside the chapel I found the boxes that the men had delivered. I moved from one to another, lifting the lids. The first contained nothing but dirt. The second one was also full of dirt. Each one, the same.

I slowly lifted the lid of the last one, expecting to see dirt there as well. My mouth opened in horror. The Count!

Dracula was lying on a layer of dirt, either dead or asleep. His eyes were wide open, but he was not breathing. I could not detect a heart-beat. In his eyes I saw a look of such evil hatred that I could bear to look at him. I lowered the lid of the box and hurried back to my own room.

It was late June. In a few days, it would be June 29, the date of the last letter.

"Soon, we must part, my friend," the Count told me. "You will return to your homeland, beautiful England. But perhaps someday I will see you again at Castle Dracula."

"Soon, you say. Why can I not go now?" I asked, testing him.

"You can, if you wish," the Count said. "You're free to go any time you like."

I hurried to the front door, which had always been locked. I was surprised to find it was now unlocked. I started to pull it open. As it creaked open a crack, I heard the howls of the wolves. They rushed toward the door, their teeth gleaming. I saw that I could not hope to outwit the Count. I could do nothing but wait. For what?

The next day, when it was light, I again cross the ledge and climbed into the window of the Count's room. Again I went down into the ruined chapel. Again I found Dracula lying in his box. He looked younger. His mustache was no longer white. His face was fleshed out and looked less pale.

I'm helping this creature to move to London, I thought. There he will find all the victims he wants. I can't do it!

Over by the wall I spotted a shovel. I lifted it and swung the blade down at that horrible face. But the eyes of the Count blazed so brightly that they made me miss my aim. Or they somehow turned the shovel aside. The metal only gashed Dracula's forehead. The lid of the box then fell shut.

My ears perked up. Someone was coming!

I ran back up the stairs to the Count's room. Below I could hear the doors creak. The gypsies had arrived to take away the boxes. I heard them hammering the lids shut. I heard them groaning as they lifted the heavy boxes. I heard the door slam closed again. I heard the sound of the key in the lock.

Now, I thought, I am alone in the castle with those awful women! Those devils!

I knew I had to get out. And quickly. I ran to the window. I will not stay here, I thought. I will creep along the ledge until I find a way to escape. Or I will die trying!

Goodbye, Mina! I whispered to my beloved. Then I stepped out onto the ledge.

Chapter 4

Mina Murray would never have dreamed that the man she loved was at that moment trying to escape from the castle of Count Dracula. She had just received a letter from him saying that he would be leaving Transylvania soon and coming home. She was looking forward to seeing him when he arrived back in England. She couldn't wait to hear his stories of the strange countries he had visited. Once they were married, she hoped, they could travel through Europe together.

To pass the time until Jonathan's return, she went to visit her friend, Lucy Westenra. Lucy and her mother were spending the summer by the seashore. They were living in a rented house in the town of Whitby, on the coast of the North Sea. Mina had finished with her duties as assistant schoolmistress and needed a vacation. She always found the sea so refreshing, and Whitby was a lovely old town.

Lucy met Mina at the railroad station. Her friend looked sweeter and happier than ever, Mina thought. They had been best friends ever since they were little girls, so it was easy for Mina to guess that Lucy had some good news to tell her.

"You and I have always shared all our secrets," Lucy said. "I have something that I'm just dying to tell you. But I'll wait until you get settled."

The two young ladies would be sharing a room in the house. Once Mina was settled, Lucy said, "You must come with me to my favorite spot."

They walked through the streets and Lucy led her friend up a hill that overlooked the town. The view was beautiful.

On one side was a beautiful green valley. Just below them, they could see the red tile roofs of the old houses. The harbor was crowded with fishing boats. The blue sea stretched beyond.

"What's that ruined church over there?" Mina asked.

"It's called Whitby Abbey," said Lucy. "It's very old. The local legend says that a lady in white could sometimes can be seen in one of the windows."

"That's kind of spooky," Mina said.

Lucy laughed. "I know you like things that are a bit scary. Let's go visit the old graveyard."

They strolled over toward the church and walked among the grave stones.

"It's such a lovely spot here," Mina said. "I wouldn't call it scary."

"I come here often," Lucy said. "You can see the harbor and the sea. And it's always quiet."

Mina agreed it was very pleasant. They sat on a seat among the gravestones.

"But Lucy," Mina said, "don't keep me in suspense any longer. What's your big secret?"

"You'll never guess," Lucy whispered. "Three marriage proposals."

"Three? Are you having fun with me?"

Lucy shook her head. "I'm almost twenty and I've never had any proposals. Now three have come all at once. And all from the most wonderful men."

"You are so lucky!" Mina said. "Tell me quickly, who are these men?"

"The first is a doctor. John Seward is his name. He runs an asylum in London, the one beside the Carfax estate."

"The place for insane people. I know of it."

"He's very intelligent, very kind. And I'm sure he was sincere when he asked for my hand. I felt so bad refusing him."

"You refused a proposal from a doctor? Why?"

"He asked me if I loved another. I had to say yes."

"But Dr. Seward sounds like a fine person."

"Yes, he is. And Number Two is even better. His name is Quincey Morris. Guess what, Mina. He's an American. He's had adventures all over the world. He tells me wonderful stories about the places he's been. I could listen for hours. He's so good-humored and jolly. When I told him I couldn't marry him, he was disappointed but not angry. He even said he hoped always to be my faithful friend. Isn't that sweet?"

"Very nice. But come, tell me of Number Three. He's the one who's important."

"Those two, when they proposed, were confident and assured. The third was not like them. He was confused and shy about it. I was confused myself. But both of us knew we were right for each other. In a moment his arms were around me and he was kissing me. His name is Arthur Holmwood. He's very handsome and very pleasant and very everything. I love him, Mina. I told him I would marry him."

"That's wonderful," Mina said. "I can't wait to meet him."

"Unfortunately, Arthur's father is sick. He had to go home to be with him. I hope he'll be able to return soon so you can meet him."

These words reminded Mina how much she missed Jonathan. She hoped to see her beloved soon. He had written that he was on his way, but it had been several weeks since she'd heard anything more from him. She was beginning to worry. So much could have happened.

The two young ladies spent many happy days together. They climbed the hill to the abbey almost every day. They sat for hours in the pleasant graveyard, reading and talking. Other visitors came there to look out over the sea. They met one old man. He must have been almost a hundred years old. Once he had been a sailor, he said.

"You must know about the legends of this place," Lucy said to him.

"Yes, can you tell us about the White Lady?" said Mina.

"That's all fool talk," the old man said. "And I'll tell you something else, half of these graves here don't even have bodies in them."

"How can that be?" Lucy asked.

"Because they're the graves of folks who were lost at sea," he said, laughing. "They can't very well rest in peace here if they're at the bottom of the ocean."

He walked off, cackling to himself. Lucy and Mina thought he was a strange old character. To be drowned in the ocean didn't seem funny to them. Thinking of Jonathan, Mina shuddered.

Mina spent time helping Lucy plan for her wedding to Arthur. It would take place at the end of the summer.

Unfortunately, the excitement had an effect on Lucy. She took to an old habit she had of walking in her sleep. Lucy's mother agreed with Mina that it would be safest to keep the door of the girls' bedroom locked shut at night.

That way, Lucy could not have a dangerous accident. Sleepwalkers sometimes fall down stairs or walk near the edge of cliffs. Still, almost every night Lucy got up and tried to leave. She always found the door locked and she always looked for the key. The only good thing was that the weather was hot. She didn't have to worry about catching a cold by walking in her night gown.

Both girls were growing anxious as they waited for the return of the men they loved. One afternoon, Lucy said, "I can hardly stand this waiting. I feel like jumping out of my skin."

"There's a storm coming," Mina said. "That's what making you so nervous."

They could see clouds piled up over the sea like huge boulders. The distant thunder sounded very threatening. Waves were already pounding the shore.

"The fishing boats are all racing to reach the harbor before the storm hits," Mina said.

"But look at that ship," Lucy said. She pointed. "It seems like it's getting too close to the rocks by the shore."

Through the mist Mina could make out the shape of a large sailing ship. It was sailing this way and that, as if no one were steering. Was it headed for the harbor? Or would it try to ride out the storm at sea? If the weather grew any worse, it could easily crash into the rocks.

No one in the village had ever seen a ship act that way. Everyone knew that something very strange must be happening on board.

At the same time the storm was raging in Whitby, Dr. John Seward was back at work in London. He had been disappointed over Lucy's refusal. The best way to get over it, he figured, was to throw himself into his job at the asylum.

Just then, he was studying the case of a very interesting patient. The man's name was Renfield. Age: 59 years old. Physical condition: strong and healthy. Mental condition: very gloomy.

Dr. Seward knew Renfield was insane. What interested him was how the man was insane.

At times Renfield seemed quite normal. For example, he loved animals. But he had a most unusual hobby. He would spend hours grabbing flies out of the air. He also raised spiders. He would feed the flies he caught to the spiders. He seemed to get a great deal of pleasure from this.

"Why are you so interested in catching flies?" the doctor asked him.

"I love them," Renfield said, "because they give me life. Watch this."

Dr. Seward watched while Renfield grabbed a big hairy black fly out of the air. He grinned as he held it in his fist. Then he popped it into his mouth and chewed it and swallowed. He smiled.

The doctor noted this behavior in his records. He hadn't seen anything like it before. Soon most of Renfield's spiders disappeared. Dr. Seward noticed that he was making pets of sparrows that always came to the asylum. The birds feasted on the spiders.

"What I would like next," Renfield told him, "is a kitten. I want a kitten to play with and feed."

The doctor told him that he could not allow cats in the asylum. The next day he found that all of the sparrows that Renfield had tamed were gone. All the doctor found was a few feathers left and some drops of blood on his patient's pillow.

"He's eaten the birds raw," Dr. Seward said to himself. "I will have to study Renfield's madness very carefully. This is a very interesting case, indeed."

Chapter 5

Fear touched the hearts of Mina and Lucy as evening approached at Whitby. The sun lit the clouds with brilliant colors – purple, pink, violet, and all shades of gold. The air was heavy and ominous. Thick thunderclouds were gathering over the sea, turning the eastern sky almost black. It was sure to be a terrible storm.

Later in the evening the wind stopped entirely. The calm air grew very hot.

"That strange ship is still out there," Lucy said.

"Oh, Lucy, I'm so afraid for them," Mina said.

The strange vessel they had spotted earlier was the only ship they could see on the water. Its sails were white against the dark clouds.

"Those sailors are crazy," other people were saying. "The ship is sure to be wrecked when the storm hits."

In the stillness, the girls could hear sheep bleating from distant fields. They could hear a dog bark in another part of the village.

The trees whispered as the wind began to pick up. Within minutes, waves were crashing into the pier that protected the harbor. An awful wind roared like a lion. Men leaned as they walked. They were almost blown down by the tremendous gale. Then a thick fog came in and covered everything. The whole scene turned white.

The last few fishing boats managed to make it into the harbor. The people cheered each one as it reached safety. The big sailing ship did not try to come in. It rode up and down on the tremendous waves.

"She's headed straight for the rocks!" someone shouted.

"Go back!" others screamed. "Head for deep water."

Their words were lost in the wind. The fog made it impossible to see what was going on.

Waves crashed against the pier. The ship just barely missed one rock, then another. It slipped past the pier and sailed straight into the harbor.

"That's an amazing bit of sailing," one man said.

"No, it's a miracle," another answered.

The village searchlight followed the strange ship across the water until she scraped to a stop on the sand. As it ground to a halt, a huge dog jumped from the deck onto the beach. He ran straight up the hill.

"What in the world? Where's he going?"

"He's running toward the graveyard," someone said.

They all rushed toward the ship. When they reached the deck, they immediately fell back, shocked by what they saw. A man was tied to the wheel that steered the ship. He was the only human on board. And he was dead!

"That ship somehow found its way into the harbor by itself!" a fisherman said.

"It's an omen," another man said. "And not a good one."

"He has a cross tied between his hands," a third man said.

"By the smell of him, he's been dead a while. At least a couple of days," said the fisherman.

The people from the village searched all through the mysterious ship. She was called the *Demeter*, a Russian vessel. She was a cargo ship, but the odd thing was, she was carrying no cargo. All they found in her hold were wooden boxes filled with nothing but dirt.

"They look almost like coffins," one man said.

"Why would anyone ship boxes of dirt?" another asked.

A lawyer from the town came forward and announced that he had been hired to take charge of the boxes of dirt. But he knew little more about the affair than did the townspeople.

"Anyway," he said, "I have been sworn to secrecy. What I do know, I can't tell."

"What happened to that big dog?" someone asked.

"He must have run up onto the moors in terror," said a man who had been by the wharf.

The customs inspectors at Whitby were anxious to read the ship's log.

"It may tell us something about what happened."

The ship had come all the way from the Black Sea in Russia, the log said. During most of the journey, everything went smoothly.

After ten days at sea, the captain wrote about a strange event.

One of the crew, Petrovsky, is missing. The men are convinced that there's something strange going on. There's someone on board that we don't know about. Someone or something.

Some days later, one of the sailors said to the captain. "Last night during that hard rain storm, I saw a strange man walking on deck."

"What did he look like?"

"Tall and quite thin. I'm sure it was not one of the crewmen. I followed him forward. I was about to ask him who he was but he disappeared."

"What do you mean?"

"Vanished. Gone. Like that."

The men began to grumble. Some wanted to get off the ship at the nearest port. The *Demeter* is an unlucky ship, they said. Worse than unlucky. Doomed!

To calm their fears, the captain ordered a search of the entire ship. They went over the whole vessel, looking in every nook and cranny where a man could possibly hide.

"You see men," said the captain when they were done. "There is no stranger on this ship. You must not let your imaginations get the better of you."

A week later, the ship ran into more trouble. A second crewman vanished. The other men grew very afraid. About the same time, an awful storm came up from the east. The wind whipped up giant waves. The ship heaved up and down. Its sails flapped violently. No one could sleep. Everyone had to work to keep the ship afloat.

When the storm passed, the sea became suddenly completely calm. There was barely enough wind to keep them moving. During those long, still nights, two more men disappeared.

The crew didn't like it at all. They whispered to each other about taking over the ship and sailing to a port where they could get off.

Afraid of a mutiny, the captain and his mate began to carry pistols on deck. They hardly dared to sleep. Another man disappeared. Then another.

"We're almost to England now, lads," the captain said. "Let's not do anything foolish."

But to his horror he realized that there were only four crewmen left. Not enough, even, to raise or lower the sails, or to set them at the right angle. The ship was at the mercy of the wind.

If that were not bad enough, a heavy fog now swallowed the ship. They couldn't see where they were, or where they were going. They sailed for two days through the thick mist.

Tonight, the captain wrote in the ship's log, *I came up on deck to take over from the man at the wheel. There was NO ONE THERE. The crewmen are all gone now. I had to take the wheel myself. I called for the mate.*

The mate came on deck. He had a wild look in his eye.

"It's here, captain," he said.

"What's here?"

"It. I saw it last night. It is like a man, but as pale as a ghost. I stabbed it with my knife. The blade went right through it as if it were air."

The man has lost his mind, the captain figured. He's gone mad.

Then the mate said, "I think I know where this being is, captain. I'll find it if it kills me. It's in one of those boxes. I know it. I know it!"

The mate went down into the hold. The captain could not leave the wheel or the ship might have crashed onto rocks. He could hear the mate hammering, prying open the boxes.

Suddenly a terrible scream filled the air. The captain saw the mate run back onto the deck.

"Save me!" he screamed.

"What's the matter with you?" The captain tried to grab the mate, who was acting like a wild man.

"I know the secret now!" he said. He instantly leaped onto a railing and threw himself into the sea.

In cramped handwriting, the captain wrote, *Now I know the secret, too.*

The inspectors turned the page of the ship's log. The next entry was short. It was the last one in the book.

Now I am alone on board. The Demeter *is doomed.*

Last night I saw It. It or Him, I don't know which word is right. I would like nothing more than to follow the mate overboard. But I have sworn to stay with my ship. I will tie a cross to my hands. The fiend does not dare touch a cross.

But I am growing weaker and weaker. It is almost night. That's when he comes out. That's when I must be alert. But I can't stay awake forever. I know that now. The horror is too much for me. The horror. The horror!

I think I hear him moving now. I hear steps. I pray to heaven that . . .

That was the end of the log.

"What does this all mean?" one inspector asked.

No one knew what to make of it. They gave the brave captain a hero's funeral. The dog, who was the only survivor of that awful voyage, was never seen again.

Everyone agreed that the case of the doomed ship *Demeter* would remain a mystery forever.

Chapter 6

Mina shook with fear every time she heard a crash of thunder. The storm had raged all night. Fortunately, Lucy slept through it all. Twice she got up and walked around the room in her sleep. Mina was careful to keep her friend from going out.

The next morning the two girls went down to the harbor to see if the storm had done any damage. Huge waves were still crashing against the shore, but the day was bright and sunny.

"I'm so glad that Jonathan wasn't at sea during that awful storm," Mina said.

"Oh, yes, it would have been dangerous," Lucy agreed.

But where was Jonathan? thought Mina. Was he safe? Why had he been delayed? Why didn't he write?

In the village, they came upon the funeral of the Russian ghost ship's captain. The townspeople carried him up the hill and buried him quite near the girl's favorite seat in the graveyard.

"Let's not stay here," Mina said. She was afraid the sad event would give Lucy more bad dreams.

The poor girl did seem upset. What happened the next day made both of them even more nervous. The old man they sometimes talked to in the graveyard was found there among the stones. Dead. His neck had been broken.

"He must have had some terrific fright," the doctor said. "It caused him to fall backward. He hit his head, twisted his neck, and was killed. The look on his features was awful to see. It was as if he had stared into the face of Death itself."

"Let's go for a long walk," Mina suggested that day. She wanted to take Lucy's mind off all these upsetting events.

"We can hike to Robin Hood's Bay," Lucy said.

"That's a good idea. It will be a lovely walk and it will tire you out so that you can sleep soundly."

They walked a long way up the coast, breathing the fresh sea air. They ate a big lunch at an inn near the Bay before starting back to Whitby. By the time they returned they were both completely tired out. Lucy seemed much healthier, though. She had fine color in her cheeks. That night, she went right to sleep.

But in the middle of the night, a horrible sense of dread roused Mina from sleep. The room was so dark that she could not see Lucy's bed. She felt she must check on her friend. She tiptoed across the room and felt the blankets.

Empty!

Mina lit a match and looked around. Lucy was gone!

Mina didn't want to wake Lucy's mother, who had been very ill herself. She quickly searched the room. Lucy wasn't there.

She looked in the sitting room that was connected to their bedroom. Lucy was not to be found. Mina dressed quickly.

"She can't have gone far," she said to herself. "She's only wearing her nightdress. Maybe she went downstairs." The front door was standing partly open. It made Mina shiver to think of Lucy wandering outside in only her nightdress. She grabbed a heavy shawl and ran out after her.

The air outside was chilled. The clock struck one with a heavy iron CLANG! Not a soul was stirring. A bright full moon lit up the town. Black clouds, driven by the wind, suddenly covered the moon, casting everything into deep shadow.

Searching frantically, Mina noticed a figure in white far up on the hill. She ran in that direction. From that distance, Mina could just make out the abbey and the graveyard. She could see the white form lying across the seat where she and Lucy always sat. The snowy figure stood out in the moonlight. As the shadow of another cloud swept over the scene, Mina could see that someone was bending over the form on the bench. Was it a man? Or was it a big dog on his hind legs? She couldn't tell. All she knew was that she needed to get there as quickly as she could.

She ran through the empty town. It seemed like she would never get there. Up and up the hill she went. Once she slipped and fell, skinning her hands on the pavement. She climbed to her feet and ran on.

Finally she approached the graveyard. She could see that the form in white really was Lucy. The same dark figure was still bending over her body.

"Lucy!" Mina shouted. "Oh, Lucy! Watch out!"

The figure looked up. He had a white face and red, gleaming eyes. It was a horrible face. Mina ran around the church toward the graveyard entrance. When she reached Lucy, the poor girl was stretched on the seat. She was all alone. No one else was in the graveyard. Had Mina been imagining that awful creature? Where could he have gone?

Lucy was sleeping, but not peacefully. She groaned and her breath came in gasps. She pulled the collar of her nightdress around her throat and shuddered as if she were freezing. Mina knew her friend would catch her death of cold if she stayed out in the chill night. She wrapped the warm shawl around her and fastened it with a safety pin. She must have pricked the skin of Lucy's throat as she did so. The sleeping girl put her hand there and groaned again. How stupid of me! thought Mina.

Mina took off her shoes and put them on Lucy's feet. She smeared her own feet with mud so that, in case they met anyone, it would look as if she were wearing shoes. It would be indecent to be going out barefoot in public.

She gave Lucy a gentle shake to wake her up.

"Where am I?"

Mina explained to Lucy that she'd been sleepwalking. She didn't mention the graveyard or the figure she'd seen.

"Mina, please don't tell anyone! Especially Mother. She has a weak heart. The shock could make her ill. Could even kill her."

"Don't worry. The secret is safe with me."

When they reached the house where they were staying, Lucy went back to bed and slept deeply. Mina was happy that when she woke her friend in the morning, Lucy was not suffering from a cold. She was usually tired out after sleepwalking, but today she said she felt very healthy.

"I've actually never felt better. I have a sense that a great weight has been lifted from me."

"That's wonderful," Mina said, "Lucy, I have to admit I was very clumsy last night."

"What do you mean?"

"When I was fastening the cloak around you, I jabbed you with the pin. There's a little pin prick on your neck. In fact, there are two of them. And you'll see there's a bit of blood on the collar of your night-shirt."

"Don't think anything of it," Lucy said. "It doesn't hurt. I forgive you."

Mina hoped Lucy's sleepwalking was over, but it wasn't. Mina locked the door every night and made sure to wear the key on a string around her wrist. She was determined that Lucy would not go out again.

Mina was having trouble sleeping herself. She kept waking up, worrying about Lucy. Once she awoke and looked across the room. Lucy was sitting up in bed. She was pointing toward the window. Brilliant silver moonlight streamed through the window. Mina crossed and looked out the window where Lucy was pointing.

"It's only a bat, dear," she said.

I've never seen one so big, though, Mina thought. She watched it flit here and there, just outside the window. It hovered close, as if looking inside at the two girls. Then it flew off. Mina watched it as it went up the hill toward the old abbey and the graveyard.

The next night, Mina couldn't sleep at all. She decided to go for a walk. She was careful to lock the door after she went out. She took a stroll around town in the bright moonlight. As she was returning home, she noticed Lucy leaning from her open window. Mina waved her handkerchief to get her friend's attention. She didn't want to shout and wake people up.

Lucy did not wave back.

"She's sleepwalking again," Mina said to herself. "She should not be so close to the edge of the window."

As Mina hurried back to their room, she thought she noticed a very large bird of some kind perched on the window sill near Lucy.

Lucy was back in bed when Mina returned. As she slept, she clutched her hand to her throat. Her face was very pale.

"I still have no news from Jonathan," Mina told Lucy the next day. "I can't imagine what has held him up. His letter said he would surely be back in England by now."

"Maybe he's seeing the sights along the way," Lucy suggested.

"I hope that's it. I can't help worrying, though."

She didn't tell Lucy that she had another serious worry. Lucy was clearly ill. She was growing weaker every day. The roses in her cheeks had faded. She had trouble breathing and was always tired.

Every night, Lucy walked in her sleep. She almost always went to the window and leaned out.

Mina could see that the wounds from the pin pricks had not yet healed. It must be because of Lucy's weak blood. If anything, the marks on her neck had gotten larger. Once, they had even started to bleed again.

At that same time, the lawyer who had charge of the boxes of dirt that had been found on the Russian ghost ship sent them up to London.

"I was instructed to ship them to Carfax Estate," he told the local magistrate.

"But why? Why would anyone pay to ship dirt?"

"I haven't the foggiest notion," he said. "I just did what I was hired to do. They are to be placed in the old chapel on that estate and left there. That's all I know. I'm glad to be done with the job. Something was very strange about it, I think. Very strange."

Soon afterward, Lucy recovered. Mina was glad to see that her friend was back to being her old self again. She had new energy and seemed so much healthier.

"Let's go back to the place we used to sit in the graveyard of the old abbey," Lucy suggested. "The air is so fresh up there. I used to love to go there."

"Do you really think you're well enough to climb the hill?"

"Yes, I'm sure of it. Come on, Mina. It will be lovely."

They walked up and sat under the trees on their usual bench, looking out at the sea.

"Do you remember coming up here the night you wandered out?" Mina asked. They had not talked of that strange night before.

"I don't remember a thing. You know I never have any memory of what happens when I walk in my sleep."

"Did you dream anything that night?" Mina asked.

"I think I remember a dark man. A very strange man with red eyes. And I heard the sound of voices, like women singing. My soul seemed to float out of my body and rise into the air. It was quite pleasant, floating along like that. But all of a sudden, I was in an earthquake. The ground was shaking. And I awoke and found it was you shaking me to wake me up."

"Does it bother you now to think of it?"

"Not at all," Lucy said. She laughed. "Why would I be bothered by a silly dream?"

Mina was glad to see that her friend's cheeks were pink again. It was the old Lucy.

The very next day, the news Mina had been waiting for finally arrived. She received word from Jonathan!

"What does it say?" Lucy asked before Mina could even read the letter. "How is the dear boy?"

Mina read the message quickly. "I was afraid of this," she said.

"Afraid of what? Don't keep me in suspense, Mina."

"He's ill. That's why he couldn't write. The letter is from a nurse in a hospital in Transylvania."

"Read it to me," Lucy said. "Tell me everything."

Mina read the letter out loud. It was in English but obviously written by a foreigner.

Dear Madam,
Mr. Jonathan Harker not strong enough to write for himself. He is getting better each day, glad to say. He is suffering from very bad brain fever

past six weeks. Has had terrible shock. He keep talking of wolves and say he been poison. Talk about ghosts and demons. He going need a long time, get better. What a sweet and gentle person he is. Us here at hospital pray every day he get better. Will take time.
Sincerely yours,
Sister Agatha

"I will go to Transylvania myself," Mina declared. "I will make plans to leave immediately. Jonathan needs me. I'll nurse him back to health. As soon as he's strong enough, I'll bring him back to England."

She made her plans as quickly as she could. Within a few days she was setting off on the long journey to Transylvania.

Just at that time, the boxes of dirt were delivered to the Carfax estate in London. The old place was next door to Dr. Seward's insane asylum. One of his assistants had just reported to him about the patient Renfield.

"I'm afraid he's growing worse, doctor."

"What's he been doing?"

"He gets excited very easily. He sniffs the air, just the way a dog does."

Dr. Seward noted this change in Renfield's file. "What else?"

"He's always nervous. He keeps repeating the words, 'The master is at hand.'"

"Is he still obsessed with flies and spiders and birds?"

"No. In that regard, he's better. Only those words, over and over. 'The master. The master. The master.'"

"Very strange. We must keep a close eye on him. He may become violent."

That night, at two o'clock in the morning, the night watchman rushed into Dr. Seward bedroom and woke him.

"It's Renfield," the watchman said. "He's escaped!"

Chapter 7

We must find Renfield before he can leave the asylum grounds," Dr. Seward told the watchman. "Alert all the guards. Alert everyone. Renfield is a dangerous man. Make sure the police are on the lookout. I'm going outside to search for him."

He was afraid what would happen if that madman made it past the fence that surrounded the asylum. There was no way to predict how violent he might be.

Dr. Seward ran out into the dark grounds that surrounded the asylum. He didn't see any signs of the madman. Whenever he thought he had spotted him, it turned out to be a wisp of fog or a flash of moonlight, nothing more.

"There he is!" one of the guards shouted.

Dr. Seward ran toward him. He caught a glimpse of Renfield climbing the high wall at the far end of the grounds. He would soon be in the old Carfax estate next door. He was already halfway up the stones, climbing it as easily as a spider goes up a wall.

"Stop! Stop him!"

Dr. Seward ran toward the place where Renfield had gone over. One of the guards found a ladder. The doctor grabbed it and climbed over the wall himself. Renfield was just ducking around the corner of the big manor house. Dr. Seward jumped down and followed him.

When the doctor rounded the corner, Renfield was nowhere in sight. A cloud suddenly blotted out the moon, casting everything into darkness. Dr. Seward felt his way carefully along. Where could the lunatic have gone?

A few minutes later, he heard a sound. It was like the whimpering of a wounded animal. He followed it. It became louder as he approached the old chapel beside the house.

Renfield was pressing against the door of the chapel. He was talking to himself.

I must approach carefully so as not to scare him, thought Dr. Seward. I dare not disturb him until the guards arrive.

He slowly crept closer until he could hear what Renfield was saying.

"I am here to do your bidding, Master. I am your slave. I will do anything for you. Anything. Command me, Master."

What is he talking about? Dr. Seward wondered. And who is he talking to? What new delusion has come over him.

When the guards finally arrived, Renfield shrank back in fear. They tried to grab him, but he fought like a wild beast. The guards had to force him into a straitjacket, tying his arms at each side. They led him back to the asylum and chained him to the wall of a padded room. There he sat murmuring, "I will be patient, Master. Someday I will join you."

Dr. Seward thanked the guards for their help.

"Renfield is more violent than ever," he said. "No telling what harm he might have done if he had gotten away. He could easily have killed people."

While all this was going on, Mina was on her way to Transylvania. It was a difficult journey for a girl to make on her own. She crossed the channel by boat, then took a long, long train ride through many countries. I don't care how far it is, she told herself. As long as I find Jonathan at the end of the journey.

She did find him, but he was not the Jonathan she remembered. He was thin and pale and very weak. When she asked him to tell her what had happened, he could not remember. He had been sick, but that couldn't explain everything. Something strange had happened to him.

"Darling, you must have had a terrible shock of some kind," she said.

The nurses told her Jonathan had spoken about dreadful things,

"What things? What were they?"

They only shook their heads. They would not say.

"Mina, my dear," Jonathan told her. "I keep trying to remember what's happened to me, but each time I think about it, my head spins around. I don't know if it was real, or if I was dreaming, or if I went mad. I hope that you will not abandon me. I hope you will still agree to be my wife."

"Of course, my love," she answered. "I will never leave you again. I've sent for the chaplain. We can be married this very day."

And they were, right there in the hospital. As soon as the wedding was over, Mina sat down and wrote a letter to Lucy back in England.

> *Dearest Lucy,*
>
> *Delightful news! I am now Mrs. Jonathan Harker. I am so happy. I have looked forward to this day for so long. I'm only sorry you could not be here with me.*
>
> *I wish Jonathan could talk about his awful experiences. It would do him good, I think. He tries, but he gets mixed up. Then he can't even remember what day it is, or even what year. I think that he's getting better little by little. I pray that his progress continues and that I may be a good wife to him.*
>
> *I hope that when you marry Arthur you will be as happy as I am at this moment. I must go and tend to my poor husband.*
>
> *Your dear friend,*
>
> *Mina*

Lucy read this letter with great joy. She missed her friend terribly, but she was happy for her, happy that she had found Jonathan, happy that she was married.

Lucy's stay in Whitby was nearly over and she was feeling much better. She no longer walked in her sleep. Arthur came to visit her by the sea.

"Lucy, you have such a good appetite that you will soon be getting fat," he joked. They played tennis and went fishing together. In another month, they would be married, too. Lucy hoped that Mina would be back in time for the wedding.

When she returned home to London, Lucy began to feel odd again. Her bad dreams returned. At night, she tried to keep herself from going to sleep so that she would have no more nightmares. She was totally worn out and could hardly drag herself out of bed.

One night she woke to hear sound at the window.

"What is it?" she said out loud. No one answered.

She listened. It was a scratching noise. Then a flapping, like a bird's wings. She grew weak and pale. Deathly pale. She tried to breathe but could not get enough air.

Looking in the mirror the next day, she saw that the marks on her throat, where Mina had pricked her with the pin, were back. They were always sore now and sometimes oozed blood.

Arthur stopped by to see his fiancee. He was shocked.

"Lucy, you must see a doctor," he said. "I am going to call our friend, John Seward. I'll get him to come over tomorrow. He'll know what's the matter with you."

Arthur couldn't stay. He had to go home to see his father, who was ill again and might die soon.

Dr. Seward came to Lucy's house and examined the sick girl. Her appearance alarmed him. She had changed so much since the last time he'd seen her, when he had hoped she would marry him. Now she was weak and tired and pale as a ghost. She seemed to lack blood.

"I'm so tired, John. Every time I lie down, I have these awful dreams."

But Dr. Seward could not find any cause for her illness. The sickness was very mysterious. Dr. Seward, who loved Mina almost as much as Arthur, was worried.

He told her, "I will contact my old teacher, Professor Van Helsing. I'll ask him to come here from Holland. He's one of the smartest scientists I know. You'll like him. He's a kind and generous man."

I pray that he can tell what's wrong with Lucy, he thought.

Dr. Seward returned to the lunatic asylum. His patient Renfield continued to puzzle him. Sometimes the man was crazy and violent. Other times he calmed down and became quite peaceful. He would be agitated all day, then grew calmer at night.

"I think he's well enough to get along without the straitjacket," he told one fo the guards. "But always keep a close eye on him."

They removed the restraint. But that night, a guard came running.

"Renfield has escaped again!" he told the doctor.

"Let's head straight for the Carfax Estate. He seems to be drawn to the place."

Sure enough, they found him at the entrance of the old chapel. When the guards tried to take him back to the asylum, he fought them. They struggled to bring him under control.

Then mysteriously, he calmed down. Dr. Seward saw him looking into the sky toward a big black bat.

"Don't worry," Renfield said to the guards. "I'll come with you quietly."

When Dr. Seward went to visit him in the morning, Renfield had gone back to his old habit — he grabbed flies out of the air and ate them, smiling and licking his lips afterward.

"My Master is gone," he said. "Without him, I must get life on my own. I must draw it from these little creatures."

What in the world does he mean? Dr. Seward wondered. If I could figure out what makes him act this way, it might open a new understanding of the human mind.

Unfortunately, he didn't have time to worry about Renfield. Professor Van Helsing had just arrived from Holland. After greeting him at the asylum, Dr. Seward took him straight to Lucy's house.

The professor's bushy eyebrows tangled together in a frown when he saw the patient. He greeted her warmly and they talked about her life and her recent visit to the seaside. The professor never mentioned her illness.

While he spent time with Lucy, he said little. Dr. Seward knew it meant that he was thinking very deeply. Van Helsing was not just a medical man. He had studied philosophy. He knew about the occult and about many other strange things.

"What do you think, Professor?" Dr. Seward asked when they were alone.

"Strange. Very strange. I must say that in all my years, this is one of the strangest cases I have ever seen. She has lost a great deal of blood. But how? It seems impossible. It's a most fascinating case, indeed. I'm glad you called for me."

"What should we do now?"

"I must go back to Holland to take care of business. I'll return as soon as I can, in a few days at the latest. I have some books in my library that may shed light on Lucy's condition."

"What can I do here?"

"Keep a close watch on the patient. If she gets worse, send for me at once."

"What could be causing these terrible changes in her, Professor?"

"I'm not sure. We will have to study her case very carefully. Right now, I can't rule anything out. Let's look at all the evidence."

"Do you agree that it's serious?" Dr. Seward said.

"Yes, most serious. I'm afraid it is a matter of life and death. What I want you to do is to pay attention to every little detail. The smallest thing could be a clue to what's troubling poor Lucy."

"I don't think we should tell her mother how bad it is," Dr. Seward said.

"No, don't say a word to her. From what you've told me, a shock could be too much for the old lady's heart. Besides, there's nothing she can do. We just have to wait and hope Lucy gets better."

Dr. Seward kept a close watch on Lucy, but she did not get any better. When Van Helsing returned after a few days, Dr. Seward took him up to Lucy's room. Both men were shocked by what they saw.

Lucy looked like a ghost. She was deathly pale, like a creature drained of blood. The color had gone even from her lips. The bones of her face stood out, as if she were a skeleton. She could only breathe with great pain. She lay motionless on her bed. She did not even have the strength to speak.

"This is awful," Van Helsing said. "The poor girl will soon die from lack of blood. We must do something and do it quickly."

Chapter 8

We have to hurry!" Van Helsing said. "Lucy must receive a transfusion of blood as soon as possible. One of us must be willing to donate."

"It has to be me," Dr. Seward said. "I'm younger and stronger. I'll be glad to do it if it will save her."

"Prepare at once. I will bring up my bag. I have all the necessary equipment."

They were getting ready to drain blood directly from Dr. Seward into Lucy's veins. Before they could begin, they heard someone pounding at the front door. It was Arthur.

"I came as soon as I could," he said. "I am grateful to you for helping Lucy, Professor Van Helsing. How is she?"

"You have arrived just in time," Van Helsing told him. "She is very ill, desperately ill. But it's in your power to help her. If we act quickly, we may save her life."

"What can I do?" Arthur cried. "I would give the last drop of my blood to save her."

"We don't ask for that much," Van Helsing said. "But the young lady needs blood right away. She needs blood or she will die. We will perform a transfusion. We will take your blood and direct it into her empty veins."

"I'm glad I am to do it," Arthur said. "Very glad."

"Then prepare immediately," the professor said. "We must hurry. She doesn't have much time left."

Lucy was not asleep, but she was too weak to talk. She spoke to her beloved Arthur with her eyes, but that was all.

The two doctors connected a tube from Arthur's vein to Lucy's. As the blood began to flow between them, the doctors saw the sick girl begin to get better. Arthur grew pale and weak, but Lucy showed color in her cheeks at last. She was only partly restored. She remained very weak.

When the transfer of blood was finished, Van Helsing told Arthur to go home and rest. "You need to eat plenty of food and restore yourself. You will quickly regain your strength. I'm happy to tell you the operation was a success. You have saved Lucy's life. I'm sure she will never forget what you have done."

Dr. Seward let Arthur out. When he returned, he found Van Helsing looking closely at the two marks on Lucy's throat.

"Have you seen these wounds?" the professor asked him.

"I have noticed them, yes."

"What do you think has caused them?"

"She mentioned something about being pricked with a pin," Dr. Seward said, looking closer. "But they have never healed properly. I thought maybe this was where she lost blood. But if that were true, her bed would have been soaked with it. There's never been more than a few drops. I can't figure it out."

"This may be even more serious than we thought," Van Helsing said. "I will have to return to Holland again and consult my books. You must stay here with Lucy. I warn you, you must not sleep at night. Not a wink. Do not let the girl leave your sight no matter what."

"Why?" Dr. Seward asked. "What danger is there?"

"I cannot say just yet. But I must beg you not to disregard my warning. Stay with her every second. If you leave her, the result may be very serious. It may be fatal!"

That night, Dr. Seward sat up in Lucy's room. The next morning she awoke. The transfusion had helped. She felt better. She was still weak, but she was on longer on death's doorstep.

"I will need to stay with Lucy again tonight," Dr. Seward told her mother.

"I don't see why, Doctor," Mrs. Westenra said. "Lucy's much improved. You are so tired. Why not go home and rest?"

"We have to trust Professor Van Helsing," Dr. Seward told her. "I do not dare leave your daughter alone until he returns. He was quite clear about it."

Lucy was still tired. But that night, Dr. Seward saw that the girl was trying to keep her eyes open.

"Why don't you relax?" he asked. "Sleep will do you good. You've been through a terrible ordeal."

"I'm afraid to sleep. Sleep is a horror to me!"

"What do you mean?" he said.

"Nightmares! Awful nightmares come to me. They seem so real."

"Don't worry about that," he said. "I'll be here with you all night. If I see any signs of bad dreams, I'll wake you at once. You can sleep in peace. There's nothing to worry about."

"Thank you, John. That's very kind of you."

She went to sleep and slept peacefully all night. In the morning, she felt better. It looked like she was on the path to recovery.

Dr. Seward had to take care of his business at the insane asylum during the day. By the next evening, he was so tired he could hardly keep his eyes open. He had not slept during the past two nights. Yet he knew he had to return to sit with Lucy.

"Don't be silly, John," Lucy said. "You don't have to stay here again tonight. I feel so much better. Lie down in the next room. Get some rest. If I want anything, I will call out and you can come in at once."

Dr. Seward agreed. He did need rest. He would lie down, but not go to sleep. He stretched out on the sofa in the next room. But as the minutes dragged on, his eyes slowly closed. Soon he was fast asleep.

Early the next morning, Professor Van Helsing arrived back from Holland. He found Dr. Seward asleep. Waking him, he asked, "How is our patient?"

"She's much better," Dr. Seward said. "She's been making steady improvement."

"Let's go see."

They entered Lucy's room. Van Helsing took one look at her and his mouth dropped open. "Oh, my God!"

Lucy was stretched out in bed, barely breathing. Her skin was whiter than the sheets. She was weaker than ever. Her gums had shrunk back from her teeth. She looked as if she were almost dead.

"All our efforts have been undone!" Van Helsing said. "Quick, before it is too late. She needs another transfusion."

He set up his equipment and began to drain blood from Dr. Seward into Lucy's veins. The doctor was glad to do anything he could. He loved Lucy, too. He felt guilty about not staying awake all night. The transfusion brought some color back to Lucy, but it left Dr. Seward feeling weak and dizzy.

"Don't mention this to anyone, especially Arthur," Van Helsing told him. "Go and eat a big breakfast. You need to rest. We have much work to do."

"Professor, how could she have lost so much blood? Where did it go? There is no sign of bleeding, only those two pin pricks on her throat."

"I can't answer that now, but I have my suspicions. We will talk later."

Lucy awoke. She was very weak, sicker than she'd ever been. Professor Van Helsing told Dr. Seward that he would stay with Lucy tonight himself.

"Do you have any idea what could be causing this illness?" Dr. Seward asked. "I have never seen anything like it."

"I'm not surprised, Doctor. If I'm right, this is not a disease you will find in any of your medical books. It's something very ancient. Very dark."

That was all he would say. That night, Van Helsing sat at Lucy's bed-side. He studied her face very closely.

In the morning, the professor went out and had a bunch of white flowers sent to Lucy.

"Why, Professor, how kind of you," she said to him when he returned. "I love flowers."

"They are not just a pretty gift," he said. "Smell them."

She sniffed them and laughed. "You're playing a joke on me. These are flowers of the common garlic. They certainly don't smell very sweet."

"I never joke!" Van Helsing snapped. His jaw became firm and his eyebrows joined together in an angry frown.

"But why garlic?" she asked.

"These flowers have a very serious purpose. And when I tell you to do something, you must never disobey me! Never!"

Lucy was startled by his anger.

Seeing that he had frightened the girl, Van Helsing became more gentle.

"I ordered garlic for your own good," he said. "It's a kind of medicine. The smell is not good, but it will have a good effect. Trust me."

Then he went around the room, putting garlic everywhere. He fas-tened the windows tightly closed and wiped garlic all around them. He hung some over the door and at each side of the fireplace. He even made a ring of garlic and hung it around Lucy's neck.

When Doctor Seward arrived, he was surprised.

"What's the meaning of this, Professor?" he said. "It seems like you're working a spell to keep off evil spirits."

"Perhaps I am," Van Helsing answered. To Lucy he said, "Take care that you do not remove this necklace. Don't open any of your windows tonight. You must promise me that."

"I promise," Lucy said. "Thank you both for all that you've done."

As they were leaving, the professor said to Dr. Seward, "Tonight we can both sleep in peace. She will be safe. Nothing can harm her if she follows my instructions."

"This is very strange, Professor. Garlic? How can that make such a difference?"

"I'm still studying the evidence, John. There are a few more things I must learn about before I'm certain. Then we will discuss the whole matter."

That night, Lucy drifted off to sleep. At first, the smell of the garlic bothered her. But gradually it gave her a sense of peace. She was no longer afraid of the awful nightmares that had bothered her for weeks.

In the morning, Dr. Seward and Professor Van Helsing returned to Lucy's house early. Her mother was very cheerful.

"Lucy looks so much better," she said. "She's still sleeping, but I looked in on her. She seems so calm. I know she needs her rest. I am so grateful to both of you."

"Wonderful," Van Helsing said. He rubbed his palms together. To Dr. Seward he said, "My plan is working. I think we may be close to finding the cause of poor Lucy's illness."

"I think I helped, too," Lucy's mother said. "I deserve some of the credit."

"How do you mean, madam?" the professor asked.

"I've been so worried about Lucy. Last night, I went in to check on her. She was sleeping very soundly. The sound of the door opening didn't even wake her. But the room was terribly stuffy and there were those awful, strong-smelling flowers all over the place. She even had them around her neck. I was sure that in her weakened state the smell would be too much for her, so I took them away. And I opened the window to let in some fresh air. I am sure you will be pleased to see how much good it's done her."

The old lady went off to have her breakfast. Dr. Seward could see that the professor's face had turned pale.

"Oh, no!" was all Van Helsing could say.

Chapter 9

I am very afraid!" Professor Van Helsing cried. "What has the mother of this poor girl done? We cannot let her know it, but she may have put her daughter's body and soul in the gravest danger."

"What are you talking about?" Dr. Seward said. "What danger can there be in opening a window?"

"There is no time to explain," Van Helsing said. "Come with me. We must hurry. We must go to Lucy this instant. It may be too late already."

Van Helsing took his medical bag. He and Dr. Seward rushed up the stairs. They came to the bedroom where Lucy was sleeping. They entered. Dr. Seward was shocked by Lucy's appearance.

"Oh, my God!" he said.

Her skin was again deathly pale. She looked like a figure made from wax.

"I'm not surprised," said the professor.

"But what has caused this awful change?"

"I'll tell you later. Right now, another transfusion is needed and it must be done this instant. You are too weak from the last time. I must give her my own blood, old as I am."

Dr. Seward performed the transfusion, hooking a tube from Van Helsing to Lucy. As the professor's blood flowed into her veins, the girl's color came back a little. Her breathing became more regular.

Lucy's mother was very upset by her daughter's condition. Van Helsing explained that she must never remove anything from her daughter's room without asking him.

"The scent of the garlic flowers is part of the treatment," he said. "It will make the girl better."

But Van Helsing was afraid to leave Lucy alone. He himself stayed with the sick girl. His presence comforted her and let her sleep in peace.

"Professor, I'm beginning to feel as if I've been through a long nightmare," she said after two days. "I've finally awakened."

"What do you remember, Lucy?"

"Fear. Terrible fear. But it seems distant now." She described the flapping against her window, the voices in her ears at night, the orders she imagined someone giving her.

"Was any of that real, Professor? Or did I just imagine it?"

"The human mind is very mysterious," Van Helsing said.

"I'm even beginning to like the smell of garlic. It makes me feel safe somehow."

Professor Van Helsing remained in her room, but he was worn out from lack of rest. That night, Lucy awoke to see that he had drifted off to sleep himself. Something was making an angry flapping sound against her window pane. She felt the old fear return. She clutched her garlic necklace and closed her eyes.

The next morning, Dr. Seward came by. He was glad to see that Lucy was improving. He joined Professor Von Helsing for breakfast.

"Strange things are happening in the city," Dr. Seward said.

"Tell me about them," said the professor.

"There was some trouble at the London Zoo. The keeper was alerted to a terrible howling from the wolf's cage. He ran to see what was the matter. Standing by the cage was a tall, thin man with a mustache. He wasn't doing anything, just watching the animal. The keeper reported that he was a nasty-looking man with a cold expression and red eyes."

48

"This is very interesting. Tell me more."

"The keeper instantly disliked the man. He told him to move back, that he was upsetting the animals. I would never do that, the man said. When he smiled, the keeper saw that his teeth were very sharp."

"Exactly!" said the professor. "Then what?"

"The man moved closer to the wolf's cage and thrust his hand right inside it. Instead of attacking, the wolf lay down. The man scratched him behind his ears. I am used to wolves, he told the keeper. I love them."

"Who was this man?"

"The keeper had never seen him before. He asked him if he kept a zoo of his own. No, the man said, but I have several pet wolves. I understand them. They trust me. Then he tipped his hat and left."

"Very strange indeed."

They talked about Lucy's condition. Both were satisfied that she was making progress. But neither of the men could guess what would happen next. Or how horrible it would be.

That night, Lucy went to bed as usual. Knowing she would keep the garlic flowers always around her, Professor Van Helsing thought it was safe to let her sleep alone.

In the middle of the night she woke up and heard the familiar scratching and flapping at her window. It was the same sound she had been hearing since her days of sleepwalking in Whitby.

She was afraid to go back to sleep. Her awful nightmares might return. She lay terrified in her bed, unable to move.

She tried her hardest to stay awake, but she felt more and more drowsy. I shouldn't stay here alone, she thought. If I drift off, who knows what might happen?

She went to the door of her room and called out, "Is anybody there?" No one answered.

From outside in the shrubs she heard a howling sound. Was it a large dog? No, its voice was deeper and fiercer than any dog. Lucy went to the window and looked out. She could see nothing. Then a big bat swooped up against the glass. It startled her, but it could not get in.

She hurried to climb back into bed. A minute later the door creaked open. Lucy pulled the covers over her head and closed her eyes, terrified.

"Are you all right, darling?" It was her mother.

"I was afraid, Mother."

"I heard you call out and I got worried," her mother said. "I came to see how you were."

"You'll catch your death of cold out there, Mother. Climb under the covers with me." They pulled the blankets up and tried to comfort each other. Lucy was so scared, she was shaking.

Then the flapping came at the window again. Her mother cried, "What in the world is that?"

Both of them heard the low howl from the shrubs. Then suddenly the window glass shattered!

The wind blew into the room, hurling the curtains back. An enormous gray wolf had burst through the window into the room.

Lucy's mother screamed in fright. She grabbed for something to fight off the wolf. Her hand caught the necklace of garlic flowers that Van Helsing insisted that Lucy wear. She tore it off.

She sat up in bed and swung the garlic at the ferocious wolf. The animal hesitated, snarling and showing his teeth. Then Lucy's mother made a gurgling sound in her throat. She fell over as if struck by lightning.

Her head knocked into Lucy's and left her daughter dizzy for a moment. The room spun around. Little flecks of light came in through the window. Lucy tried to move but could not. She was frozen in place.

Her mother lay on top of her. When Lucy looked at her mother's face, she had an awful shock. The old lady was dead!

Lucy swooned. She remembered nothing more for a while.

When she awoke, it was still the middle of the night. Lucy could hear dogs howling all over the neighborhood. A bell was tolling. From outside came the beautiful song of a bird. Lucy imagined that it was the voice of her dead mother.

Two maids now came running into the room. They had heard the commotion. They were shocked to see that their mistress was dead.

They lifted Lucy's mother off the bed and laid her body out on the couch, placing a sheet over it.

"Bring me those flowers," said one. "I'll put them near her."

The other maid handed her the broken necklace of garlic. Lucy remembered what Van Helsing had said, but she couldn't bring herself to remove the flowers from her poor mother.

She didn't think there was reason to worry now. Surely, the maids would stay to keep watch over her mother's body. But the two servants went out and never returned.

Lucy went to look for them and found them in the kitchen. They had drunk some sherry to soothe their nerves. It must have contained a sleeping potion. They were both fast asleep!

Lucy hurried back to her room to sit with her dead mother. The broken window let in a draft of cold air. From outside, she heard the low howl of the wolf. She became very afraid. Yet there was nothing she could do.

She sat there shivering, waiting for whatever horrors were in store for her.

Chapter 10

The next morning Dr. Seward and Professor Van Helsing walked over to Lucy's house together.

"More strange news," said the doctor. "Remember that wolf we were talking about yesterday? He escaped from the zoo!"

"No!" the professor exclaimed. "How did it happen?"

"No one knows. After the zoo closed, the keeper was passing his cage and found the bars twisted open. Yet nobody had been in the zoo after they locked the gate."

The keeper put out the alarm, Dr. Seward went on, and the police said all children in the city should stay indoors. "But what was even stranger, the wolf returned at daybreak. He had been cut in several places and they could see broken glass sticking through his fur."

"I don't like the sound of that," the professor said. "I think we should get to Lucy as quickly as we can."

They hurried to Lucy's house. Dr. Seward pounded on the door. They waited. No one answered.

"I fear we are too late," the professor said. "Hurry! If we cannot find a way in, we must break in."

They went all the way around the house, looking for a way to get in. At the back of the house they were able to force open a kitchen window and climb into the house. They found the two servants still sleeping. They did not stir.

"It appears they've taken some kind of sleeping potion," Dr. Seward said.

"Quickly!" Van Helsing. The doctors sprinted up the stairs to Lucy's room.

What a sight they saw! Lucy's mother lay on the couch. Her face was twisted in an expression of horror. Her eyes were wide open, but she was dead!

Lucy was stretched across her own bed. Her skin was utterly white. The two wounds on her throat looked raw. They were oozing blood. The professor ran over to listen for her heart beat.

"It's not too late!" he cried. "She's still alive."

"She has to have yet another transfusion of blood," Dr. Seward said.

"Yes, but first we must warm her," Van Helsing told him. "She is almost as cold as her dead mother. Prepare a hot bath at once."

Dr. Seward woke the maids from their deep sleep. They quickly heated water for a bath. They carried Lucy to the warm water and soaked her in it.

While they waited for her to warm up, Dr. Seward said, "I am afraid this is a life or death struggle, Professor."

"It's worse than that, Doctor. Much worse. If it were only natural life we were talking about, we could let Lucy die in peace. This is something more serious, more dangerous by far."

"What can be more serious than death?"

"You'll see. We are not dealing with something natural here. This is much darker than anything you know about."

Lucy's heart began to beat a little more strongly as the maids dried her off with hot sheets.

"There's still a flicker of hope," Van Helsing said.

At that moment, they heard a knock at the door. Quincey Morris, Arthur's American friend, had come bringing a message from Arthur. Arthur's father was very ill and he needed to stay at the old man's bedside. He wanted to be with Lucy, too, and had sent Quincey to see how she was doing.

"You are just in time," Dr. Seward said. "She needs a transfusion. Both Professor Van Helsing and I have given too much of our blood already. Can you do it?"

"Or course," Quincey said. "To save Lucy I'll do anything. As you know, I also love that young lady and wanted to marry her."

The two doctors prepared for the transfusion. They ran tubes from Quincy into Lucy's arm and let the blood flow. After the operation, Lucy was better, but only slightly. She was still pale and her breathing was shallow.

"How is it possible?" Quincey asked when the operation was over. "How could she receive the blood of four strong men in a matter of days and still be so pale and weak? Where did all that blood go?"

"I can't even begin to guess," Dr. Seward said. "This is one of the deepest mysteries I have ever come across."

That afternoon Lucy finally awoke. She looked around the room, trying to figure out where she was. All of a sudden she gave a loud cry and began to weep.

"She has remembered, no doubt, that her dear mother is dead," Professor Van Helsing said.

There was nothing the men could do for the poor girl. She remained in low spirits, sobbing in her grief. About sunset she fell into a light sleep. All night the two doctors took turns watching her. She slept, but often moaned or called out as if she were having a bad dream. Quincey Morris walked around outside of the house. He carried a pistol in his pocket and was prepared to shoot if the wolf returned.

In the morning Lucy had not improved. She seemed weaker. She could hardly turn her head and would eat almost nothing. She had a hard time keeping her eyes open. Frequently she drifted off to sleep. Dr. Seward noticed how worn out she looked.

"Look, Professor," he said. "Her teeth have changed. They appear longer and sharper than usual."

"Yes," said the professor. "I'm not surprised."

They sent a telegram to Arthur. He rushed back to London. He was shocked when he saw Lucy's face. He wanted to stay with her every minute.

"You must get some rest," Van Helsing told him. "You've been under an awful strain yourself and we may need you later."

They had moved Lucy into another room where they could lock the window. Again, the professor put flowers of garlic everywhere, draping a necklace of them around Lucy's neck.

As Dr. Seward sat with the poor, sick girl, he noticed that her teeth were even sharper than in the morning. The two canine teeth were longer than the rest and pointed like fangs.

What could it mean? What was happening to this poor girl?

In the middle of the night, he heard a flapping sound at the window. He went over to see what it was. A huge bat, larger than any he'd ever seen, was scraping against the glass. It seemed to want to get into the room. Very strange.

He returned to Lucy. She was restless. In her sleep, she had torn the garlic from around her throat, as if she couldn't stand it. He tried to replace it, but the necklace was broken.

At dawn, Van Helsing came to relieve Dr. Seward.

"How has she been?" he asked.

"Not good, Professor. She sleeps but does not rest." He told the professor about the bat.

Van Helsing took a careful look at Lucy and gasped.

"Hurry," he said. "Open the curtain. I need light."

Dr. Seward drew back the curtain. He rushed back to the bedside. Van Helsing was examining Lucy's throat. "Look!" he said. "Look at this."

He pointed to Lucy's throat where the two wounds had been. They were gone. There was no sign of them.

"What does it mean, Professor?" Dr. Seward asked. "Is she getting well at last?"

"No, she is dying! There is no more hope for her. All that matters now is whether she dies awake or asleep. Contact Arthur and tell him to come right away."

Alarmed, Dr. Seward hurried to where Arthur was still asleep downstairs.

"Call on all your strength now, my friend," he said. "I'm afraid that the end is near for Lucy."

"No!" Arthur exclaimed. "I can't believe it's true!"

They rushed back up through the house. When they reached Lucy's room, they found that Van Helsing had brushed her hair and made her look a little like her old self.

"Arthur my love," she whispered. "Come near."

With tears in his eyes, Arthur sat near Lucy's bed. He held her hand as she drifted off to sleep. Her breathing became heavy. Her mouth fell open a little and Dr. Seward again noted her long and pointed teeth.

When she awoke once more, she said, "Kiss me, Arthur. Please kiss me."

"No!" Van Helsing said.

"I beg you!" Lucy said.

Arthur leaned forward, but the professor grabbed him by the neck and pulled him away. "You must not kiss her! Never!"

Arthur was startled. What could this mean?

Lucy's face changed. She looked at the professor and whispered, "Thank you. You are a true friend. Protect him from evil. From me."

"I will."

"And, when the time comes, please give me peace."

"I'll do it. I swear I will," Van Helsing told her.

To Arthur he said. "Kiss her once, but only on the forehead."

As Arthur leaned over to kiss her pale forehead, Lucy's breath grew harsh again. Then it stopped.

"She is dead," Van Helsing said.

Dr. Seward led Arthur into another room. When he returned, he found Van Helsing studying Lucy's face. Relaxed in death, finally at peace, she looked almost as beautiful as she once did. All the suffering that had marked her face during her weeks of her illness had vanished.

"Well, poor girl," Dr. Seward said, "at last you are at peace."

Van Helsing turned to him and with a grave and solemn voice said, "No, you are wrong. She is not at peace. This is only the beginning!"

Chapter 11

Dr. Seward made arrangements with the undertaker for Lucy and her mother to be buried together the next day.

He and Professor Van Helsing then read Lucy's diary and letters, searching for clues about what might have happened to her and why she died.

They looked through the papers all day. As night fell, Van Helsing said, "We should go and get some rest. We still have a great deal of work before us."

Before they went to bed, they entered the room one more time where poor Lucy's body was laid out. The undertaker had left a sheet over Lucy's face. When Van Helsing lifted it, both he and Dr. Seward drew back in surprise.

"I can't believe my eyes," Dr. Seward said.

All of Lucy's loveliness had come back to her. Not a trace of illness remained. Professor Van Helsing rubbed his hand across his mouth. A very grave and worried look came over his face.

"Doctor, I must ask you to stay here until I return," he said. "This is not what it appears."

He rushed out. When he came back, he had an armful of garlic flowers. He mixed them with the other flowers that they had ordered to be placed near the corpse. Then he took a small gold cross and laid it over her mouth. He pulled the sheet back to cover her face.

"I've always thought of you as a sane and reasonable man, Professor Van Helsing," Dr. Seward said. "But everything you've done has been mysterious. The garlic, the crosses. What does it mean?"

"Have I ever done anything without a reason?" Van Helsing asked. "I know you were surprised when I would not let Arthur kiss his beloved. But remember, Lucy thanked me for it. You must trust me, John. There are strange and terrible days before us. We have to work together, even though I cannot explain everything now."

Dr. Seward took Van Helsing's hand and promised to help him any way he could. The next day, just before the funeral Arthur came to look once more on the woman he loved.

"How beautiful she is!" he said to Dr. Seward. "I am amazed. It's almost hard to believe that she's dead."

"I agree with you, Arthur. But I know she is."

Everyone who saw her was astounded by Lucy's appearance. She seemed to grow lovelier by the hour.

Arthur kissed Lucy's hand and kissed her on the forehead. Then the undertaker put the lid on the coffin and screwed it in place.

In Exeter, many miles to the west of London, Mina and Jonathan Harker, who were now husband and wife, had just been to another funeral. Mr. Hawkins, the lawyer who Jonathan worked for, had died.

"The business is mine now," Jonathan said. "It's going to keep me very busy."

"I know you'll do well, my dear," Mina said.

Soon afterward, Jonathan had to go to London to see about some legal matters.

"Why don't you come with me," he said to Mina. "You'll enjoy a short stay in London."

Indeed, Mina did like to go to the city. The second evening they were there, she and Jonathan went walking along the street to look in the windows of all the shops.

"It's wonderful to see all the lovely things for sale," Mina said. "I just wish – ow! Jonathan, you're hurting me."

He was gripping her arm so hard that it was painful.

"My God!" Jonathan said. His eyes were bulging from his head.

"What is it?"

"Look!" He was staring at a tall, thin man with a black mustache. "Do you see who it is?" Jonathan whispered.

"No, dear, I don't know him," Mina answered. "Who is it?"

"It's the man himself! It's the Count! But somehow he has grown young. How can it be?"

"It's probably someone who looks like him."

"No! I would never mistake him. That's Dracula!"

"But nobody can grow young, dear. Unfortunately."

The man moved on but Jonathan remained very upset. Mina was afraid the brain fever he had suffered in Transylvania was coming back. But the next morning, he seemed to have forgotten all about the incident.

Mina was still not sure if the things that Jonathan had written in his Transylvania diary had actually happened. Maybe they were just products of his imagination.

It was true he had gone there to help the Count move to London. What if everything he said was true? What if Dracula was now in London? If he was really the evil force that Jonathan described, he would have millions of possible victims here. The idea of it made her very worried.

The next day, they returned home to Exeter. Mina found a telegram waiting for her. She read it, then buried her face in her hands and cried.

"What's the matter, darling?" Jonathan asked her.

"Lucy's dead!" Mina cried. "And her mother, too. I can't believe it. The funeral's today. They'll be buried together."

"How awful," Jonathan said. "Do they say what happened to the poor girl? Who sent you the telegram?"

"A man named Van Helsing," she said. "I don't know him. He says he wants to come here right away. He wants to talk to me about Lucy. It's urgent, he says."

The next day Van Helsing arrived in Exeter. Mina was anxious to meet him. She had to find out about poor Lucy. She also hoped that a professor, a man of learning, might also help explain Jonathan's strange experience and illness.

"I have read your letters to Lucy," Van Helsing told her when he arrived. "In them, you wrote about a time when you saved her from sleepwalking. You mentioned a graveyard. That interests me very much. Can you tell me all about that?"

Mina gave the professor all the details. It was the first time she had told anybody about Lucy's strange adventures.

"Your story makes many things clear," Van Helsing told her when she finished. "What you have said is very helpful in understanding this unusual case. You've been a great help to me. If there is anything I can do for you in return, you need only ask."

"There is something, Professor," Mina said. "My husband Jonathan has suffered from brain fever, which came over him when he was in Transylvania. I'm afraid that something is still bothering him. I don't know if there's anything you can do to put his mind at ease. But perhaps you might know how he could get better."

"Tell me about it," the professor said.

"I will only if you first promise not to laugh at us," she said. "The events were so strange, they hardly seem possible. More like something out of a fairy tale."

"You don't have to worry," Van Helsing assured her. "If you only knew the things that I have gone through with your friend Lucy, you would see that I have an open mind. I know that the world is filled with strange things."

Lucy told him all she knew about Jonathan's trip to Castle Dracula. The old professor was fascinated by the details and asked her many questions.

"I can promise you this," he said when she had finished. "Everything that your husband said happened, did happen. You need not have doubts about it. It is important that I speak with him as soon as possible."

"He had to go away on business," Mina said. "But I'm sure he'll be happy to see you once he returns. One thing bothers me, Professor."

"What is it?"

"If what happened to Jonathan in Transylvania is true, it means that Count Dracula is in London now. That monster is free to prey on many, many innocent persons."

"That's very true," Van Helsing said. "That's why we must take action right away. You and your husband could be a great help to many beside yourselves."

"We'll do all we can."

Van Helsing returned to London right away. He rushed to the asylum to meet with Dr. Seward.

"On the way back here, I have been reading a story in the newspaper that disturbs me very much," Van Helsing said. He handed it to his friend to read.

Several young children had gone missing in London. When their parents found them, the children told of a "beautiful lady" in a white gown.

"It says the children were healthy, but not entirely so. They were a little weak. A little pale."

"That reminds me of Lucy," Dr. Seward said.

"Exactly! We must go see these children at once."

The two men hurried over to the hospital where one of the little victims was being treated. They knew the doctor there, and he let them examine the child.

"What do you see?" Van Helsing asked.

"Puncture wounds," Dr. Seward said. "Almost exactly like those on Lucy's throat. Do you think they could have the same cause?"

"Not the same, no," Van Helsing said. "I wish that it were so."

"But what do you mean, doctor?"

"John, do you think it's possible that things can happen in the world that science cannot explain?"

"No, I don't. I am a man of science. I think everything has an explanation."

"But what about hypnotism?" Van Helsing said. "Didn't that seem strange at first? What about those bats in South America that can drain the blood of a horse?"

"Do you think Lucy was bitten by a bat? Is that what made her ill?"

"No, I only want to prepare you to believe what is very hard to believe. You said that maybe the marks on the children came the same way as Miss Lucy's wounds. I tell you, it is not so. It is far worse."

"What do you mean, Professor?"

"Those marks were made by Miss Lucy herself!"

Chapter 12

You're mad, Professor!" Dr. Seward cried. "Lucy's dead. We both know that. Dead and buried."

"I wish I were mad," Van Helsing said. "I assure you, I would never insult the memory of Miss Lucy. And you are right. She's dead. But if you come with me tonight, I will show you something that will astound you."

Dr. Seward agreed to go. Yet he could not believe that what the professor said was true. It couldn't be. And because he had loved Lucy, he wished at least that she now was resting in peace.

The two men had dinner together. Van Helsing said little as they ate. Afterward, they set out for the graveyard.

"We must enter Lucy's tomb," Van Helsing said. "Arthur gave me the key to the door."

The metal door creaked open and Dr. Seward stepped first inside the cold crypt. The flowers that had brightened the tomb for Lucy's funeral were now wilted and dead. Spiders and beetles had made the room their home. Dust had settled on everything.

They found Lucy's coffin among the others of her family. Van Helsing removed a screwdriver from his bag

"What are you going to do?" Dr. Seward asked.

"Open her coffin. That is the proof I spoke of. I would not do it, but in this case we have no choice."

He unscrewed the lid and removed it. Dr. Seward drew back and wrinkled his nose. He was afraid of the vile smell that would come from the decomposing body.

But no smell emerged.

"Look, Doctor," Van Helsing said. He held his candle down over the coffin. Dr. Seward could see that it was empty!

"What is the meaning of this?" Dr. Seward said. He was shocked.

Van Helsing put a hand on his friend's arm to steady him.

"It is just as I suspected."

"But what happened? Where is Lucy's body?"

"Why do you think the body is absent?" Van Helsing asked.

"It must be grave robbers," Dr. Seward said. "They broke in and stole it. There's no other explanation."

Van Helsing screwed the lid of the coffin back in place and they left the crypt.

"Normally, I would agree with you," he said. "But I suspect that there is an explanation, a horrible one. We must watch now. You stand on that side of the tomb, I'll hide over here. Keep your eyes open."

A distant clock struck twelve as the two men waited in the chilly cemetery. The time passed slowly. It struck one and then two. Dr. Seward shivering with cold.

Suddenly he saw a white streak moving through the graveyard. It disappeared among the shadows of the trees. Dr. Seward hurried across the graveyard to get a closer look. He tripped and fell. As he rose, he saw the white figure again. It flashed toward Lucy's tomb and disappeared.

Dr. Seward hurried back to where he'd left Van Helsing. The professor was holding a small, sleeping child.

"Are you satisfied?" Van Helsing asked. "Did you see?"

"No, I didn't," Dr. Seward said. "Only a figure in white. Where did that child come form?"

"Examine him closely," Van Helsing said.

Dr. Seward struck a match and examined the little boy's throat.

"There's no mark on him."

"Because we were just in time," Van Helsing said. "We must leave this little fellow in a spot where a policeman will find him."

They carried him to a main street. When they heard a policeman approach, they placed the little boy in the pathway and hurried on.

"That was only a hint," Van Helsing told his friend. "Tomorrow you will have your real proof."

The next day, they went out to the graveyard in the afternoon while it was still light. No one was around. Again they entered Lucy's tomb.

"Why have we come back?" Dr. Seward asked. "We both know the tomb is empty."

"You will see," Van Helsing said. He unscrewed the lid of the coffin.

Dr. Seward was again shocked. There lay Lucy, looking more beautiful than ever. Her lips were red, her cheeks rosy. She looked as if she were alive.

"But the teeth," Van Helsing said. He pulled back Lucy's lips. "They are longer and sharper than before. It is with these teeth that she has been attacking the little children."

"I can't believe what I'm seeing," Dr. Seward said. "What can possibly explain it?"

"She has become one of the Undead," Van Helsing said. "She was bitten by a vampire. That's what caused her to sicken and die. But she has now become one of them. We must kill her as she sleeps."

"Kill her? But she's already dead."

"Yes, kill her for good so that her soul will be free. We will ask Arthur and his friend Quincey to help. It will be an awful task. We have no choice."

They replaced the lid of the coffin and left the graveyard.

Back home, Dr. Seward could hardly believe what he had seen. There must be a rational explanation for all of this, he told himself. Or perhaps the strain of recent weeks had driven him insane. Driven them all insane.

The next day he and Van Helsing met with Arthur and Quincey.

"We are going to need as much help as possible in what we must do," Van Helsing said to Arthur. "Because you loved Miss Lucy, I ask you to come along. But it will be a difficult task, the most difficult of your life."

"What are you talking about, Professor?" Arthur asked. "What task?"

"We can do no harm to Miss Lucy now, because she is dead. Do you agree?"

All the men agreed.

"But what if she is not dead?"

"What on earth do you mean?" Arthur cried, jumping to his feet. "Was she buried alive?"

"No, she is neither alive nor dead. She is Undead," Van Helsing said. "We have a duty to her now, to her soul. We must release it."

"How can we do that?"

"You will see. First you must see proof, as Dr. Seward here has seen proof. You must see with your own eyes."

The four men met at the graveyard that night. Clouds made the night very dark. Now and then they let flashes of moonlight through.

The men came to the tomb.

"We were here yesterday and found Lucy in her coffin," said Van Helsing. "Isn't that so, Dr. Seward?"

"Yes, that's true."

They entered and Van Helsing opened the coffin.

"Tell me, what do you see?" he said.

The coffin was empty!

"Where is she?" Arthur demanded. "What have you done with her body?"

"Nothing," Van Helsing said. "You will see for yourself."

The men went back outside. The night air seemed fresh and healthy after the damp smell of the tomb. Van Helsing closed the door of the tomb and placed garlic all around it.

"Now we must wait," he said.

They hid and waited. Each man was terrified of what he might see. Then, through the dark, came a white figure, a woman. In her arms she held a sleeping child. Arthur started to move, but Van Helsing held him back.

The figure came closer. The moon broke through the clouds. In its light, they could see her face clearly. It was Lucy!

The four men moved in front of the door of the tomb. Van Helsing shined the light of his lantern on the woman. All of their hearts grew as cold as ice.

It was Lucy, all right. But all the sweetness in her face had turned to cruelty. She drew back and snarled at them, the way a wolf snarls. Her lips were red with fresh blood. Blood trickled down her chin and onto her gown. Her eyes were red and furious.

She took the child and flung it to the ground. She growled. The child gave a cry and lay on the ground moaning.

Lucy's lips curled back in a hideous smile. She reached out her fingers toward the man she was to have married.

"Come to me, Arthur," she sang. "Come. Come so that we may rest together. Come, my husband, come."

Her voice was as sweet as it had been in life. Arthur opened his arms and took a step toward her. Van Helsing sprang forward and held out a gold cross.

Lucy held up her arm and turned away. She ran past them toward the tomb. But the garlic made her turn back. She stared at the men with a look of hatred. Sparks came from her eyes. Her bloodstained mouth opened wide. She looked as if she wanted to kill them all.

"Do you believe me now?" Van Helsing asked Arthur and Quincey. "Do you see what she has become?"

"Yes," they agreed.

"Will you follow my instructions?"

"We will do what you say."

The professor took the garlic from around the tomb. Lucy slipped through a crack. She passed inside the grave without opening the door, as if she were a spirit.

"We will meet back here tomorrow afternoon," Van Helsing said. "We will do what we must do and give her soul rest."

The three young men, Arthur, Quincey Morris, and Dr. Seward met the next afternoon with Professor Van Helsing. Instead of his usual medical bag, the professor was carrying a long leather sack.

They barely spoke as they walked up to the graveyard. All of them entered the tomb. Van Helsing unscrewed the lid of Lucy's coffin. She lay there as if asleep.

"She's as beautiful as ever," Arthur said. "Is that really her, Professor? Or is it a demon that has taken her shape?"

"It is her body, yes," he answered. "But it is not her. Look at her teeth. Look at the stains of blood. We must get to work at once."

From his bag, the professor took some knives like the ones surgeons use. He laid them on another coffin. He drew out a wooden stake, three feet long and three inches thick. It was sharpened at one end and hardened by fire. He also took a heavy hammer.

"The Undead can never really die," he said. "They go on forever, preying on others for blood. In doing so, they turn their victims also into Undead. If Lucy had kissed you, Arthur, you too would have become Undead. The children whose blood she sucks are not yet lost. But in time they will come under her spell. We must make sure she actually dies, once and for all. Then her soul will be set free."

"Let me be the one to do it," Arthur said. "Tell me how. I will not weaken."

"It will be an awful task," Van Helsing said. "This stake must be driven through her body, her heart. Then we will cut off her head."

"Oh, no!" Arthur said, trembling as he took up the thick stake.

"Place the point over her heart," Van Helsing said.

Arthur placed the stake gently on Lucy's chest. He took up the heavy hammer.

Professor Van Helsing read a prayer for the dead. When he finished, he said, "Do it now, Arthur. Do it for her."

Arthur lifted the hammer high and brought it down, striking with all his might.

The body in the coffin writhed. A hideous screech came from the red lips. The corpse shook and twisted. The teeth clamped together, slicing the lips. The eyes came open wide.

Arthur did not stop. He drove the stake deeper and deeper. Blood spurted all around. Then the body stopped trembling and became calm. It was over.

The hammer dropped from Arthur's hand and he fell backward. He nearly collapsed from the strain.

"But look, Arthur," Van Helsing said. "Look at her now."

68

There in the coffin lay Lucy as she had been in life. Her teeth were normal. She was no longer a vampire. A calm light washed over her delicate face.

"Thank you, Professor," Arthur said. "I know she is truly at peace now."

The men sawed off the end of the stake. They cut off the corpse's head and filled the mouth with garlic, as Van Helsing instructed. Finally, they replaced the lid of the coffin and left the tomb.

"One step of our work is done," Van Helsing said. "A greater task remains."

"What is that, Professor?" Dr. Seward asked.

"We must find the vampire. We must find Count Dracula and do the same to him. We must stamp him out. It will be a difficult and dangerous business. Are you men ready?"

They all agreed they were.

"And will you do what's needed, however horrible?"

Again they said they would.

"Let us meet tomorrow to make our plans. Once we begin, we must finish the job. There will be no turning back."

Chapter 13

While these horrible events were happening, Mina and Jonathan traveled to London as they had promised Professor Van Helsing. They stayed in Dr. Seward's large house. He lived upstairs, the insane asylum was on the ground floor. That night they met with the doctor and with Arthur Holmwood and Quincey Morris.

Professor Van Helsing talked about what would have to be done. "We must track down Count Dracula," he said. "To do so, we have to study all the clues."

"What happens when we find him, Professor?" Dr. Seward asked.

"We have an awful task before us. We must rid the earth of this awful monster once and for all. We need all the knowledge and all the help we can get."

They began to look through Lucy's and Mina's letters, the diary Jonathan had kept in Transylvania, newspaper articles, anything that might give clues about Count Dracula. Where was he and what was he up to? Mina helped to examine everything and put all the facts in order.

"First," Van Helsing said, "I must tell all of you something about the enemy we will be fighting. All of you will find what I am about to say difficult to believe. But you must believe it."

"I'm ready to hear what you have to say, Professor," Mina said.

"Vampires have been around for centuries," he told them. "They are the Undead. They never die, yet they are not really alive. They are stronger than twenty men. They are very smart. They have taken on the knowledge or many centuries. When they walk in front of a lamp, they cast no shadow. When they stand before a mirror, you see nothing in the glass."

"How powerful are they, Professor?" Arthur asked.

"Very. They have power over the weather. They can create storms. They can bring on fog. They can command animals. Owls and rats and wolves obey them. They themselves can turn into a wolf whenever they want. Or into a bat. They live in the dark and can see in the dark. They can shrink until they are small enough to slip through a tiny crack. When they want, they can vanish without a trace."

"They sound like an awfully powerful enemy," Arthur said. "What if we fail to defeat them?"

"I would tell you that it is a matter of life and death," Van Helsing answered. "But it's more serious even than that. If we fail, we ourselves will become like them. Each of us will become a foul thing of the night. We will forever walk the earth, sucking the blood of the living. Make no mistake, my friends, this battle we are about to fight is a very, very serious one. Do you dare to join me?"

"I will do everything possible to hunt down Dracula," Mina said. All the men agreed with her. They joined hands and vowed to work together until the vampire was destroyed.

"This is wonderful," Van Helsing said. "Together we are strong. We can act when and where we want. Vampires are limited."

"Do you mean Vampires do have weaknesses?" Quincey Morris asked.

"Most definitely," Van Helsing said. "They must have blood to live. Vampires do not eat ordinary food. Jonathan will remember that he never saw Count Dracula eat or drink. It is blood they must have. When they suck the blood of the living they grow strong. They become younger, even. But without this blood, they become very weak."

"What other weaknesses do they have, Professor?" Quincey asked.

"A vampire cannot enter a house unless someone inside invites him to come in. However, once he's been invited, he can return to that house any time he wants."

"Very strange," said Arthur.

"A vampire is only powerful at night. He is a creature of the night. When day comes, he loses all power and must rest. If he is not at home, he must return to a coffin that contains earth from his native land. That is why Dracula had the boxes of dirt sent from Transylvania."

"So he has a refuge here," said Dr. Seward.

"Dracula can only change himself into a wolf or bat at sunrise or sunset, no other time. He is afraid of water and can only pass over a body of water with the help of others."

"What are our defenses against him?" Mina asked.

"Very good question," Van Helsing said. "Some things can take away his power. Garlic is one. Also, sacred symbols like the cross. In the end, we must drive a stake through his heart and then cut off his head. It's the only way to kill him so that he becomes truly dead, never to rise again."

"But who is Dracula really?" Jonathan asked the professor.

"The Dracula family is a very old one in Transylvania," Van Helsing explained. "Count Dracula was a great warrior who fought against the invasion of the Turks. But he practiced black magic. The devil captured his soul and turned him into a vampire. This happened centuries ago. I fear that—"

Suddenly they were all startled by a pistol shot that crashed through the window.

"What was that?" Arthur cried.

Dr. Seward jumped up and ran to the window.

"It's Quincey!" he shouted.

None of them had noticed when Quincey had quietly gotten up and left the room. They waited for him to return, which he did right away.

"Sorry to startle you," Quincey said. "I went outside because I saw a very large bat hovering at the window. I hate those horrid things."

"Did you hit it?" Arthur asked him.

"I don't think I did. It flew away into the woods. It was headed toward the Carfax estate."

They continued talking about ways of tracking down Dracula.

"I've found something interesting in these records," Mina said. "Fifty boxes of earth were taken from the ship in Whitby. Do you know where they were shipped to? To Carfax estate, right next door!"

"So Dracula has been living close by," Arthur said.

"Maybe that explains the strange behavior of my patient Renfield," Dr. Seward said. "At times he acts sane and reasonable. Other times he grows wild. Several times he has escaped and run over to the Carfax Estate. He called out, 'Master! Master!' Once he attacked several work-men who were removing packages from Carfax."

"What type of packages?" Van Helsing asked.

"Big wooden boxes shaped like coffins."

"Do you know what that means?" the professor asked the others.

Dr. Seward said, "It probably means that Count Dracula is preparing other places around London to hide. That makes our job of finding him much more difficult."

"The first thing we should do," Arthur said, "is to go over to Carfax and see how many boxes are left there."

"Certainly," Van Helsing said. "And we must go tonight. But it is we men who will do it. Miss Mina should stay behind."

"No, I should go along too," Mina said. "I'm just as ready to hunt vampires as any man."

But the men wouldn't hear of it. "You stay behind, darling," Jonathan told his wife. "You'll be safe here."

As the men were preparing to go over and search the estate, one of the asylum guards ran in.

"Dr. Seward, the patient Renfield demands to see you right away. He says it's urgent. He's acting very strange."

"I think we should see what he wants," Dr. Seward told the others. "He may give us clues to the movements of the Count."

All four men went down to Renfield's room. Dr. Seward introduced the others to his patient, who was sitting calmly on his bed.

"Arthur Holmwood," Renfield said. "I knew your father. I was sorry to hear of his death. Mr. Quincey Morris, I understand you come from Texas. You should be proud to call such a great state home. And Professor Van Helsing, what an honor to meet a famous scientist like you. I have read all of your books."

The others looked at Dr. Seward curiously. This man was no lunatic. He appeared completely normal. Dr. Seward wanted to warn them that other times Renfield had acted sane one minute, then turned into a madman in an instant.

"What was it you wanted to see me about?" Dr. Seward asked Renfield.

"I wanted to ask you to let me leave here," Renfield said. "As you gentlemen all can see, I am no more insane than any of you. There is no reason to keep me locked up."

"Perhaps," Dr. Seward said. "Certainly I'm glad you're making progress. We can consider later whether it's time for you to return home."

"No, I mean tonight," Renfield said. "Right away. It's terribly important that I do not stay in this asylum a second longer. I ask you this not just for myself. It is important for a much larger reason."

"What is that?" Dr. Seward asked

"I'm afraid I can't tell you."

"It wouldn't be wise for you to leave us just yet," Dr. Seward told him. "We need to make more observations."

Renfield became excited. "Please, Doctor," he said. "I beg you. You don't have to take a chance. Send guards with me if you must. Put me in a straitjacket if you think I'll become violent. But let me leave this place. I assure you, on my word of honor, I am not insane now. Can't you see that? I am a man fighting for his soul."

"I'm sorry," Dr. Seward said. "It's impossible. We must go now. We will talk in the morning."

"You are making a terrible mistake," Renfield shouted. "You'll see! You'll learn!"

The men left Renfield's room. They finished their preparations and set out for the dark and mysterious estate next door.

Chapter 14

I must warn you, my friends," said Professor Van Helsing. "Our mission is a dangerous one. Our enemy is very powerful. Our chance of success is uncertain. Dracula can break a man's neck with no effort. He can attack in many ways. We cannot hurt him in any ordinary way. We must find him, but we must not allow him to touch any of us. Take these things for your protection."

He handed to each of them a little silver cross and a necklace of garlic blossoms.

"Keep the cross near your heart," he said. "Put the flowers around your neck. Never remove them."

Quincey Morris brought his pistol with him, though Van Helsing assured him it would have no effect on Dracula. They also brought lanterns and a set of keys. When they arrived at the door of the big house next door, Dr. Seward tried several keys. He finally found one that opened the lock. The rusty hinges of the door creaked as they pushed it open.

"Don't let that door close all the way," Arthur said. "We don't want to be locked in in case we need to get away in a hurry."

The light from their lanterns threw great shadows against the walls as they moved around the room. The floor was coated with dust. Tangles of spiders' webs hung from the walls. On a table, they found a ring of keys.

Jonathan had studied maps of the estate when he was helping Count Dracula to purchase it. He led them to a solid oak door with iron bands that closed off the old chapel. They used one of the keys to open it.

"What is that awful stench?" Quincey Morris asked.

The odor in the room was noxious. It smelled of something dead. It also reeked with the pungent smell of fresh blood. The stench of the foul air made the men sick. All of them drew back, ready to run outside. But they had no choice. They had to continue into that sickening place.

Their first task was to count the wooden boxes of earth. The coffins were scattered around the floor of the chapel. Twenty-nine of the fifty boxes were there. That meant that almost half of them had already been moved somewhere else. Count Dracula could be living in any one of them.

"We must search this place. Look for any clue about where the other boxes have gone," Van Helsing said.

They split up and began to examine every part of the chapel. For a moment, Jonathan thought he saw a familiar face. He cowered back in horror from the red eyes and pointed teeth of Count Dracula. But then the face disappeared without a trace.

Quincey Morris heard a rustling sound on the floor. He shined his lantern down to see what it was. Rats!

"Look!" he whispered to the others. "They're everywhere."

Hundreds of crawling, gnawing rats had appeared in the chapel. Soon their bodies covered the floor in a thick, writhing mass. Their evil little eyes shined in the light of the lanterns.

"I thought we might have a problem with rats," Arthur said. "I came prepared." He took a silver whistle from his pocket and blew it.

Three terrier dogs came running over from Dr. Seward's house. At first they wouldn't enter, they only stood at the door and howled. But once Arthur lifted them over the doorway, they went to work. They chased the rats around, grabbing them in their jaws and killing as many as they could. They soon cleared the whole chapel. The place seemed fresher now, as if an evil presence had departed.

The men continued on. They searched the main house at the Carfax

Estate but found nothing that would tell them where Count Dracula might be hiding.

"It is nearly dawn," Van Helsing said. "We must go home now."

Back at Dr. Seward's house, Jonathan noted that Mina was a little paler than usual.

"How are you feeling, darling? I hope you haven't been worrying about me too much."

"I'm all right," she said. "Perfectly fine."

They all slept late after their ordeal. Even Mina seemed to feel the strain. She was still sleeping after Jonathan got up. When he called her, she looked at him for a moment as if she didn't recognize him. There was almost a look of terror in her eyes.

"Whatever is the matter, my dear?" Jonathan asked.

"I've been troubled all night," she said. "I've seen some strange things."

"What were they?"

"First an odd streak of white mist moved toward the house. Then that patient downstairs, Mr. Renfield, began to make noise. He seemed to be arguing with someone, but I couldn't understand the words. I thought I heard a struggle or a fight. I was so frightened that I crept into bed and pulled the covers over my head. I must have had bad dreams because I'm more tired than if I had not slept at all."

"The problem is that you've been worrying too much about this business with Count Dracula," he told her. "It's made you nervous. Try to forget about it. We will avoid talking of Dracula in front of you."

"No, you're wrong," she said. "You were wrong to leave me out. I'm sure of that."

During the morning, Van Helsing went down to see the patient Renfield. Was he really sane now?

Renfield was acting very differently than he had been the night before. He sat on his bed and would not answer questions. He called Van Helsing "you silly Dutchman." He had even gone back to his old ways. Van Helsing watched him spread sugar on his window sill in order to attract flies. The ones he caught he immediately popped into his mouth and swallowed.

He certainly is insane, Van Helsing said. Dr. Seward is right to keep him locked up.

Jonathan and the others went out to try and find what had become of the twenty-one boxes of earth that Dracula had already moved from his estate. Jonathan talked to the two workmen who had helped move the boxes.

"We delivered them to a house in the center of London, wasn't it, Freddy?"

"'At's right," the other said. "The Piccadilly section, it was."

"A skinny old man let us in."

"He even helped us move the boxes. I remember thinking at the time, this bloke is strong. I couldn't believe he could carry those big boxes of dirt. He made it look like they weighed nothing at all."

Jonathan reported this to the others. Van Helsing said, "The Count is very smart. As long as he has a box of his native soil to hide in, we will never be able to find him. We must go to this house in Piccadilly at once. Soon he will move the boxes to even more places."

"What if we find the boxes, Professor?" Quincey asked.

"We place garlic on them during daylight. That is when Dracula is weakest. We must make it impossible for him to return to these coffins."

That night, Jonathan asked Dr. Seward to look at Mina.

"I'm a bit concerned," he said. "She's been so weak and tired lately. I think the strain of vampire hunting is too much for her. She should have stayed home instead of getting mixed up in this."

Dr. Seward examined Mina and noticed how pale she had become. She was very tired and her eyes drooped.

"You must eat better and get more rest," he said. "You've been working way too hard, arranging all the documents about the case. Try to get a good night's sleep and worry about nothing."

Dr. Seward returned to his office to take care of the business of the asylum. While he was working, one of the guards from the asylum came pounding on Dr. Seward's door.

"You must come quick, Doctor!" he cried. "Renfield has had a terrible accident!"

Chapter 15

Dr. Seward ran down the stairs and threw open the door to Renfield's room. What he saw shocked him. The patient was lying on the floor in a large pool of blood. Renfield was badly injured. His face was black and blue and looked as if it had been beaten against the floor.

"I think his back is broken," the guard said. "He can't move his right arm or leg."

"Help me to lift him onto his bed," Dr. Seward said.

They lifted Renfield carefully and laid him on the bed.

"I don't understand this at all," the guard said. "He may have beaten his face against the floor, as I've seen madmen do. But then how did he break his back? It's impossible."

"Don't worry about that now," Dr. Seward said. "Run and tell Dr. Van Helsing to come here at once. Hurry!"

Van Helsing came and examined the patient. "We must operate soon or he will die," he said.

"I agree," said Dr. Seward. He sent the guard away. He didn't want him to hear what Renfield might say if he woke up.

"His skull is broken, too," Van Helsing said. "Even if the operation saves his life, he might not be able to talk. We must find out what happened to the poor man."

A minute later, Arthur and Quincey came running into the room. "We couldn't sleep," Arthur said. "We heard the commotion and came running. What on earth happened to Renfield?"

"I hope we will find out," Van Helsing said. "If it's what I think it is, there is grave danger for all of us."

He and Dr. Seward prepared to operate on Renfield's head.

"The patient is barely breathing ," Dr. Seward said. "He could die at any moment."

"There is no time to lose," Van Helsing said. "His words may save many lives."

They operated quickly, trying to repair the damage that had been done. When they finished, all four men waited for Renfield to awaken. They sat beside him for more than an hour. Then, quite suddenly, the patient opened his eyes and looked around wildly.

"Where am I?" he said.

"Stay calm, Renfield," Dr. Seward said. "You're in your own room."

"I've had the most awful dream. Why does my face hurt so much? Why can't I move my arm?"

"Tell us your dream," Van Helsing said.

"Dr. Van Helsing, how good of you to be here," Renfield said. Again he seemed like a normal, sane person. "I call it a dream, but I know that it was no dream. It really happened. I know, too, that I only have a few minutes before I die. Or worse."

"Tell us what happened," Van Helsing asked him again.

"Promise me you won't let me become one of them! No matter what happens, you must save my soul."

"We will take care of everything," the professor said. "But you must tell us about your experience."

"It began that night when I begged you to let me go. I wanted to explain then, but I did not dare to speak about it. After you left, he came to me. He was there, at the window."

"Who came?" Dr. Seward said.

"Who? Who do you think? Dracula! He was laughing at me. I could see his red mouth and his sharp white teeth. He wanted me to ask him to come into the house. I wouldn't at first. I was afraid. But he promised me things. I couldn't resist."

"What did he promise?" Van Helsing said.

"Life," Renfield murmured. "He said I could have all the flies I wanted, big fat ones. And spiders. And rats. Rats, rats, rats! he said. Hundreds and thousands of them. All full of red blood, full of life. He showed me the yard outside teeming with rats, all their little eyes glowing red like his."

"So you let him in?" Dr. Seward asked.

Renfield struggled to speak. "I couldn't help it. I opened the window and said, 'Come in, Master.' He was inside in an instant. Then, I waited for him to send me the rats. But he didn't. Instead, only he showed up. Every night he was here. He entered without even knocking. He sneered at me. Fool, he called me. Insane fool."

"Why did he come?" Van Helsing asked. He could see the patient was near death.

"Why?" Renfield said. "For her. For Mrs. Harker, the beautiful woman who lives in this house. I saw her today. She has changed. Haven't you seen? She is pale, as if her blood has drained out. And why? Because Dracula has been stealing the life from of her."

All the men became tense. They suddenly realized that Mina was in grave danger. They trembled to think that she would follow Lucy to an early grave — or worse.

"When he came tonight, I was ready," Renfield went on. "I'm not a coward. I grabbed hold of him. You know, Professor, that madmen have tremendous strength. Sometimes I am mad. I used all my power to hold him. I would not let him get to her again. I thought I could keep him from harming her anymore. But then he turned his eyes on me. Those awful eyes! They burned into me. They made me weak. He lifted me up and threw me onto the floor over and over. Everything went dark. The last thing I remember is a mist seeping under the door into the asylum."

"This is bad!" Van Helsing said. " It means that Dracula is here right now, in this building. And we know why. To attack Mina! But we must hurry. It may already be too late. Every second counts. Let's prepare and go to her!"

The four men ran back to their rooms and gathered their crosses and garlic flowers. They met in the hallway outside of the Mina's room. She and Jonathan were asleep inside.

"Do you really think we should disturb them at this late hour?" Quincey Morris asked.

"We must," Van Helsing said.

They tried the door. It was locked.

"We have to break it down," Van Helsing said. "At once!"

Dr. Seward and the others threw themselves against the door. It burst open and they all fell into the room.

They looked around. What they saw made them stop dead. The hair stood up on their heads. Each man's heart pounded in his chest.

In the moonlight by the window, Jonathan lay on the floor. He seemed to be asleep. Mina was kneeling on the edge of the bed. Her nightdress was smeared with blood. By her side stood a tall figure dressed in black. It was Dracula! He was clutching both of her hands in one of his powerful hands. He gripped the back of her neck with the other. He was pressing her face against his bare chest.

Dracula turned toward the men. His eyes glowed red with hatred. His sharp teeth clacked together like those of a wild animal. He threw Mina roughly back onto the bed and leaped toward the men.

At the same moment, all of them held up their crosses. The Count stopped dead in his tracks. The men came toward him, their crosses held out. A cloud blotted out the moonlight for an instant, making the room go dark. When the light returned, Dracula was gone.

Mina let out a horrible scream. She was as pale as death. Her lips and cheeks and chin were all smeared with blood. Her eyes were mad with terror. Her hands still bore the marks of Dracula's powerful grip.

Dr. Seward put her in bed and covered her up. Arthur and Quincey ran to look for the Count. A minute later, Jonathan awoke.

"What happened?" he asked. "What is wrong with Mina? What does all this blood mean?"

"Do you remember nothing of what happened?" the professor asked.

Jonathan thought. He pulled at his clothes as the memory returned. The others told him what they had found. Told him about Dracula.

"Professor Van Helsing and Dr. Seward," he said, "you must guard Mina while I go out and look for him. I will kill him! I swear it!"

"No, Jonathan," Mina cried from the bed. "I have suffered enough tonight. Please don't leave me."

Jonathan rushed over to hug his wife. But when she saw the blood that she left on his shirt, from her mouth and from the two holes in her throat, she shrank back.

"No! I must never touch you again," she said. "I know that I am unclean. Unclean!"

Arthur and Quincey returned from their search.

"Bad news," Arthur said. "The Count found our records of the case and burned all the papers. We're back where we started."

"No, we're not," Mina said. "I made copies of everything. They're in Dr. Seward's safe."

"I checked Renfield's room," Quincey reported. "The poor man is dead. When I entered, I saw a bat fly from Renfield's window."

"Which way did he go?" Dr. Seward asked him. "Toward Carfax?"

"I wish he had," Quincey said. "I would have had a clear shot at him with my pistol. But he swerved away and went off toward another of his hiding places."

Van Helsing turned to Mina. "Now, my dear, I don't want to tax your strength, but you must tell us exactly what happened. We have no time to lose."

"I took the pill that you gave me to help me sleep," she said. "But I still didn't feel drowsy. I was afraid that one of those awful dreams might come if I dozed off. I tossed and turned in bed, then I must have finally fallen asleep. When I awoke, Jonathan was asleep beside me and the moonlight was coming in the window. Then I began to grow very afraid."

"Why?"

"I noticed a white mist seeping under the door."

"Why didn't you wake me, dear?" Jonathan asked.

"I tried, but you wouldn't wake up. It was as if you were under a spell. Suddenly, the mist became a man. He was tall and quite thin. He stood by the bed and stared down at me. He was dressed in black, but his skin was as white as can be. His sharp teeth showed between very red lips. Or course, from all our discussions, I knew exactly who he was."

"You couldn't call out for help?" Van Helsing asked.

"No," Mina said. "I wanted to, but the man told me he would kill Jonathan if I made any sound. He whispered to me, 'I am thirsty, very thirsty.' And then he leaned over and placed his reeking lips on my throat."

She buried her face in her hands and sobbed. Jonathan groaned. Mina pulled herself together and went on, "In the next moment, all my strength faded away. Finally he lifted his foul mouth and said, 'You have helped those men hunt me. Now I will make you my companion and helper. You will take the place of your friend Lucy. When I command, you will obey.'"

"What happened then?" Van Helsing asked her

"He opened a vein in his chest with his fingernails, which are like claws," Mina said. "He pressed my mouth to the wound. I had to swallow or I would have suffocated. Oh, what have I done? Why has this happened to me? I'm so afraid!"

"We were wrong to leave Miss Mina out of the hunt," Van Helsing said. "From now on, she will help us to track down Dracula."

They all agreed that this would be best.

"And if I see any signs that I am becoming a vampire myself," Mina said, "if I think I might harm those I love, I will die first. I will kill myself."

"No!" Van Helsing shouted. "You must not die. That is not the way to fight him. If you die, you will become as he is, Undead. You must live. You must struggle to live. Dracula is the one who must die. He must die for all time. We must find him and drive a stake through his heart. It is the only hope for you, the only hope for all of us."

Chapter 16

While they ate a quick breakfast, they planned their hunt for the vampire. Arthur and Quincey had gone out find where the boxes of Transylvanian dirt had been moved to.

"We were able to find three, spots," Arthur said when he returned. "The first you've already heard about. It's in Piccadilly, right in the center of London. The other two are on quiet streets in different parts of the city. Where the others are we haven't found out yet."

"We should focus on that house in Piccadilly," Professor Van Helsing said. "That was the first one he moved boxes to. It's an ideal location because he can come and go at all hours. There are always a lot of people around, so he wouldn't arouse suspicion. If we can get into that house, we may be able to trap the Count."

"One advantage we have," Dr. Seward said, "is that the Count still doesn't know how close we are on his trail."

"He doesn't even know we've examined his hideout in the old chapel next door," said Arthur.

"It's just like a fox hunt," Quincey Morris observed. "We have to find him before he goes into his borrow. Find him and kill him."

"But this is not sport," Van Helsing said.

"What's our next step, Professor?"

"We will go to all the houses we know about and put garlic on the boxes so that Dracula cannot use them for refuge. It seems almost certain he will come back to the house in Piccadilly sometime during the day. He will need to rest. We will be there waiting for him there."

"What about the boxes in Carfax?" Arthur asked.

"We will put garlic on those before we leave," Van Helsing said. "If he returns there, he will not find anywhere he can stay."

"You men will have to go on your own," Jonathan said, "I can't leave Mina alone here."

"No, you must go," Mina told him. "They will need every man to trap Dracula. You know the Count. You know more about him than anyone. No one else has talked with him. Because you're a lawyer, you can help the others get inside the house in Piccadilly. It is far more important to destroy Dracula than to stay here and take care of me."

Jonathan thought it over and agreed she was right.

Before they left, Van Helsing examined Mina carefully. She was pale, but her teeth had not yet begun to grow sharp. There was time to save her, but they would have to hurry.

"You will be safe here, Miss Mina," he said. "Dracula can do you no harm until sunset. We will return before that. But to be sure, I will leave you this cross."

He took a gold cross and touched it to Mina's forehead. She let out an awful scream. It burned her flesh as if the metal were white-hot.

"Oh, no!" Mina said, pressing her hand to her forehead. "I know what this means. I'm becoming a vampire myself. Look, the cross has left a scar."

"You may have to bear that scar on your forehead until we can find the vampire and destroy him," Van Helsing said. "But I assure you, we will succeed. We will not fail you."

When they had gone outside, the professor said to the others, "You see how important it is that we find Dracula. Otherwise, Mina will spend eternity wandering the earth as one of the Undead."

Hearing this, Jonathan secretly vowed that if Mina had to be a vampire, he too would become one. He would not leave her alone, even if it meant giving up his own soul.

The men crossed over to the Carfax estate. Inside the ruined chapel they found the same boxes of earth that had been there on their last visit. Now they placed garlic flowers and a cross on top of each box. If Dracula returned, he would have nowhere to hide and nowhere to rest.

"That's a good first step," Van Helsing said. "If we use every effort, Dracula may be dead by sundown. Then Miss Mina will no longer bear that terrible scar on her forehead. Nor will her soul be in danger."

They traveled by horse-drawn cab to Piccadilly Circus, a big open area with fancy buildings all around. Arthur and Jonathan hired a locksmith to open the door of the house that Dracula had bought. Jonathan told the man that he was acting as the Count's lawyer. The others watched impatiently, hoping that the Count would not return before they got inside.

A foul smell filled the house. They spread out to look for the boxes.

"I found them!" Quincey shouted.

"Twenty-one boxes came here," Van Helsing said. "You discovered that twelve boxes have been moved to the Count's other two houses. That means there should be nine left."

"But there are only eight here," Dr. Seward said. "He must have hidden the last one somewhere else."

"That's unfortunate," Van Helsing said. "Still, we are getting closer. Quincey, you and Arthur go to his other houses. Get inside any way you can. Put garlic and crosses on those boxes. I will wait here with Dr. Seward and Jonathan. The Count may arrive at any moment."

As they waited, the time passed slowly. Dr. Seward studied Jonathan's face. A few days before, Jonathan had been a young man. Now his hair had turned white and his face was haggard.

He's worried about his wife's fate, Dr. Seward thought. I can't blame him. It's awful to think about.

Van Helsing tried to cheer up his friends. "We are bound to be successful!" he said. "We will not let Dracula escape."

The house was very quiet. Suddenly, a knock came on the front door. Van Helsing motioned the others to be quiet. He went to the door and opened it. A telegraph boy handed the professor a message.

"Oh, this is good!" Van Helsing said.

"What does it say?" Jonathan asked.

"It is from your dear wife," the professor replied. "She says Dracula came back to Carfax. But our plan worked. The crosses and garlic repelled him. He hurried away again immediately."

"Then we will soon meet!" Jonathan said. "Good! I have a score to settle with that demon."

Another knock sounded at the door. The three men moved forward as one. Each held a cross in one hand. Dr. Seward had a pistol in the other. Jonathan held a long knife.

This time it was Arthur and Quincey returning.

"We found the other two houses," Arthur said. "Six boxes in each. "We placed the garlic and crosses, making them useless for the vampire."

"Excellent," the professor said. "We must now wait. But if it grows too late we will have to hurry back to Miss Mina. I do not dare leave her alone after dark."

The men sat down to wait. Arthur pulled out his pocket watch. The sound of its ticking filled the room.

"What's that?" Quincey whispered.

The men heard a key quietly turning in the front door. They all retreated to the dining room. Quincey Morris, who had organized many hunting expeditions, took charge. He made a quick plan of attack.

"Professor Van Helsing, Dr. Seward, and Jonathan, you stand behind the door. Arthur and I will hide near the window. We'll be ready to keep him from going out."

The men waited nervously as slow careful steps came nearer along the hallway. The Count was always on guard.

Suddenly, Dracula burst into the room with a leap. He spun around, glancing at all the men.

Jonathan immediately threw himself in front of the door and held up his cross. The Count could not escape that way.

Dracula stared at the men with a low snarl and a look of cold contempt. He bared his long, pointed teeth. The men all took a step closer, each holding a cross in his hand. Jonathan suddenly lunged forward, stabbing at the Count with his knife.

But Dracula was quick as a cat. He jumped back to keep the blade from piercing his heart. It only tore his coat. Immediately, a stream of gold coins fell to the floor with a metallic rattle.

A deep, awful hate filled the Count's eyes. His pale skin turned a sickly yellow. As Jonathan raised his knife to strike again, Dracula ducked down, slid under his arm and dashed across the room. He threw himself at the window and crashed through the glass. He fell into the yard outside.

The men all ran to the window. They looked down to see the Count standing there unhurt.

"You think you can harm me?" he said, "Fools! You'll be sorry, all of you. My revenge has just begun. You'll see!"

He turned and hurried across the yard to the stable. He passed through the stable door and disappeared.

Jonathan leaped out the window into the yard. Arthur and Quincey ran out the door. All three men sprinted to the stable. But Dracula had barred the door. By the time they managed to force it open, he was gone.

"Hurry," Van Helsing told the others. "Our efforts were good, but not good enough. Now Dracula is more dangerous than ever! We must reach Miss Mina before sunset. We absolutely must!"

Chapter 17

Tell the driver to hurry!" Van Helsing said from inside the horse-drawn cab. "There's not a moment to lose."

"Can we still defeat the monster?" Jonathan asked.

"He fears us now," Van Helsing said. "He saw our power and was in a great hurry to escape. That is a good sign. We have eliminated almost all his hiding places. Now he only has one box of earth left, one place to hide. When we find that, we can destroy him forever."

They arrived and found that Mina was safe. They told her all that had happened.

"I can't wait to drive a stake into that demon's heart!" Jonathan said. "I would give anything to do it right now."

"You must remember, though, dear," Mina said, "that Count Dracula is also a tortured soul. It's true that you will have to kill him. But you should also have pity on him."

"I will never pity that fiend," Jonathan said. "I will send his soul to hell first."

"Don't say that," she pleaded. "Remember that I, too, may need such help someday. I only hope that someone will do what's needed to free my soul. And perhaps have pity on me."

"Don't say that. It can't happen." Jonathan wept to hear his wife talk this way. But he knew it was true. She too could become a vampire like Dracula.

"Forgive me, darling," he said. "I'm not thinking clearly. Let's just hope that our efforts succeed."

"There's nothing more we can do now," Van Helsing told them. "We should all get some sleep. It's been a very long day. Tomorrow we will continue to hunt the Count. I hope we are successful at last."

They went to bed in Dr. Seward's house. During the night Mina awoke in terror.

"Jonathan," she whispered, "there is someone in the hallway."

Jonathan took up his big knife and crept to the door. When he eased it open, he saw Quincey Morris sitting outside in the hallway.

"What are you doing there, Quincey?"

"One of us will be on watch here all night. Just in case Dracula decides to return. We're not taking any chances."

When Jonathan told Mina about Quincey standing guard, she was able to sleep peacefully until just before dawn. Suddenly she awoke again.

"Jonathan," she said. "Go get Professor Van Helsing right away. Hurry!"

The professor came to her room, still in his nightshirt and robe.

"If you were to hypnotize me now, Professor, I feel that I can speak freely as the sun comes up. I can give you clues. But hurry, time is short."

Professor Van Helsing was able to put Mina into a trance quickly. At this time of day she was in tune with Count Dracula. He motioned for Jonathan to bring the others in so that they could hear.

"Where are you?" Van Helsing asked her.

"I don't know, everything is pitch black." She was seeing what Dracula saw.

"Do you hear anything?"

"Yes, I hear water lapping. And footsteps. Men are moving around. I hear a chain clanking."

The sun was completely up now. Mina lay back on her pillow. Then she awoke and asked, "Have I been talking in my sleep?"

"You told us a great deal," Van Helsing said. "The Count is on a ship. The clanking of the chain is the anchor being pulled in. That means the ship is sailing away."

"He's leaving London," Arthur said.

"Yes," Van Helsing agreed. "This is an important clue. We knew he was trying to escape us, and now he has succeeded."

"Good, we're done with him," Jonathan said.

"No, we must now plan how to follow him."

"Why follow him?" Jonathan asked. "Why not let him go?"

"Why?" Van Helsing said, very serious. "I'm surprised you would ask this. If we do not find him and destroy him, I'm afraid that Miss Mina will become as he is. We must do it for her sake. We cannot fail."

During the day, Professor Van Helsing, Quincey and Arthur all went out to investigate. They knew the Count would be returning to Transylvania, so they looked for a ship that was bound for the Black Sea. They found one, the *Czarina Catherine*.

"It sailed this morning," Arthur said. "It must be the one."

The men went to the wharf where the ship had been docked. They found a man in the office on the pier and questioned him.

"Do you remember anything unusual about the *Czarina Catherine*?" Van Helsing asked.

"Indeed I do," he said, "I remember a tall, thin man who came here and wanted to put a box on that ship. All dressed in black, he was. He sent the box over and it was put on. Then, just before the ship sailed, he came again. He said he wanted to see how his box was stowed. He wanted to make sure it was secure. He went on the ship and the crew showed it to him."

"That's all?"

"Except for the fog. It came in thick for a time. Luckily, it lifted before the ship was to set sail."

That evening, they reported back to the others at Dr. Seward's house.

"The ship is headed for Varna, a city in Romania on the Black Sea," Van Helsing said. "That means we have time."

"Time to do what?" Jonathan asked.

"To go there! If we hurry, we can reach the city by train before the ship docks."

"When we arrive," Quincey said, "we can alert the police."

"No," the professor said, "this is no job for police. We must do it ourselves. We must get aboard the ship before Dracula can reach land. That is our only hope."

The next day they made plans to travel to the Black Sea. Late in the afternoon, Van Helsing took Dr. Seward aside.

"My friend John," he said, "have you noticed the thing that I have?"

"I'm afraid so, Professor. Mina has changed. Something about the way she looks at a person. A very cold look. And she says little. She's not herself."

"You don't mention the main thing. Her teeth are much sharper. I am afraid that she is becoming a vampire more quickly than we thought she would. This is very bad."

"Somehow, the Count must still have power over her," Dr. Seward said. "That's why she can enter Dracula's mind when you hypnotize her."

"We must be very careful and watch her very closely. There could be a grave danger."

That night they met again. They made their final plans to take the train to Varna.

"The four of us will leave tomorrow," Van Helsing said. "Jonathan will stay behind to look after Mina."

"No," Mina said. "You must not leave me behind again. You see how I am, don't you, Professor?"

"Yes, I'm afraid I do."

"I'm still under the power of the Count. I can feel it."

"Don't say that, Mina," Jonathan said. "I can't bear to think that even now he has influence over you."

"It's true, my husband. I cannot help it. If he calls me, I have to go to him. It's safer for me if all of you are around to guard me. And I can help you to find him by giving you clues during the Count's journey. Every morning you can hypnotize me and look into Dracula's mind."

"She's right," Van Helsing said. "We should all go together."

Arthur and Quincey went to the station and bought the tickets. The next day they crossed the English Channel and boarded a train headed across Europe to the Black Sea.

They arrived in Varna a week later. They had plenty of time. The Czarina Catherine would not reach the port until a few days later. Arthur went to the steamship company and asked for messages to be sent to them about the progress of the ship wherever it was spotted.

Every day the same message came, "No report of ship. Her position unknown."

Every morning Professor Van Helsing hypnotized Mina. Every morning she reported the same thing as she entered the mind of the Count: "All is dark. I hear water rushing past."

The ship was still at sea, still moving toward Varna. They had time to plan.

"When the ship arrives," Van Helsing told the others, "we must get aboard her before sunset. Dracula will still be in his box until then. He can do nothing during the day. He will be at our mercy. If we can reach him in time, we will be successful."

"I've already talked with the officials," Arthur said. "In this country, a bribe can buy anything."

They waited. As each day passed, Mina looked a little paler and her teeth grew a bit sharper.

To get aboard the ship when it docked, Arthur told the customs agents at the port that something had been stolen from his friend in England. He said he suspected it was in the box on the ship. If it was, he would show them proof of ownership. To make them agreeable, he gave each a bribe.

When the box was opened, Van Helsing and Dr. Seward would be waiting. They would quickly drive a stake through Dracula's heart, then cut his head off. Jonathan, Quincey and Arthur would prevent anyone from interfering, using his pistols if necessary.

"But what about afterward?" Arthur asked. "Won't the authorities arrest us for murder?"

"Once the vampire's soul is free," Van Helsing told him, "his body will turn to dust. There will be no evidence left."

At last the message came that the *Czarina Catherine* had reached the Black Sea. It would arrive in Varna in a day or two.

"Just in time," Van Helsing told Dr. Seward. "Mina is getting worse more rapidly. I believe it is because the Count is approaching."

The men spent the day preparing. Jonathan sharpened his long knife until it cut like a razor. He was very worried about Mina. She was growing weaker every day.

The morning the ship was supposed to arrive, Professor Van Helsing was barely able to wake her. He hypnotized her as usual.

"Dark," she whispered. "Water."

Another day went by, then another.

"Where is that ship?" Jonathan asked. He was the most impatient. He wanted to end his wife's agony as soon as possible.

"She may have been delayed by fog," Van Helsing said. "It's very common on the Black sea."

Another day past and the ship still did not sail into Varna's harbor. But then Arthur burst in with news.

"I've just received word about the ship."

"What's become of it?" Quincey asked.

"It has arrived, but not here. It docked today at Galatz!"

"Galatz?" Van Helsing said. "That's hundreds of miles up the coast from here."

"What does it mean, Professor?"

"It means that Count Dracula has escaped again!"

Chapter 18

Everyone was stunned. They knew the Count was tricky, but they never thought that he could escape from them altogether. Now he was free in his home country. They were in serious danger, Mina most of all.

Van Helsing told them he had a plan.

"There is no time to lose! Arthur, you hurry to the station and buy us all train tickets to the city of Galatz. Quincey and Jonathan, you run down to the shipping officers bribe them to give us permission to board the ship as soon we arrive in Galatz. Dr. Seward and I will stay with Mina and protect her."

"The funny thing is, Professor," Mina told him. "The grip of the Count is looser now. I feel better than I did."

"It's because he has moved away from you," Van Helsing said. "He is anxious to escape us now and is not thinking of you. But you are still in danger. We must hurry to catch up with him."

Early the next morning they boarded the train for Galatz. The sun was coming up as they started to move.

"It is time to hypnotize you, my dear," Van Helsing told Mina. When she was in a trance, he asked her what she saw.

"Darkness. I still see darkness. The water is not rushing past now. It is swirling softly. I hear something."

"What is it? What do you hear?"

"A creaking sound. Like oars on a boat."

"That means he's coming ashore. I hope this train is not delayed. We may still have a chance to find him."

The train was delayed, then delayed again. They were still traveling the next morning as the sun came up. The professor tried hypnotizing Mina again.

"It's harder and harder for me to enter his mind," she said.

"Tell us anything you see or hear."

"I hear voices speaking in a strange language," she said. "I hear wolves howling. Many wolves."

They reached Galatz late in the morning. Arthur and Quincey took Mina to their hotel to rest. Van Helsing, Dr. Seward, and Jonathan hurried to the wharf. They found Captain Donaldson, the commander of the *Czarina Catherine*.

"Could you tell us about your journey here, Captain?" Dr. Seward asked him. "It's very important."

"One of the strangest I've been on," the captain said. "At first everything went well. All the way from England, we had excellent weather. The wind was behind us the whole way. In all my years of sailing, I've never made such good time on that journey. We entered the Black Sea easily and I expected to be in Varna ahead of schedule."

"What happened then?" Van Helsing asked.

"Fog," the captain told him. "One of the worst fogs I've ever run into. It was so thick you couldn't see two feet. We kept sailing on and on, but had no idea where we were going."

"Didn't that worry you?"

"It certainly did. I was afraid we might run into rocks or veer off our course. Some of the crewmen came to me and they were very upset. They said they wanted to throw overboard a box stored in our hold. They didn't like the looks of the man who had brought it aboard. I told them they had no right to do so. We had taken it as cargo and it had to be delivered."

"So you brought the box here?" Dr. Seward asked.

"We sailed through that fog for five days," the captain said. "When it lifted, we found ourselves near Galatz. We had to pull into the harbor to take on supplies."

"But the box was sent to Varna," the professor said.

"That's true, originally it was. But just before the sun came up one morning, a man arrived on board. He had orders to collect a box for Count Dracula. Everyone on the ship was happy to give it to him."

"What was that man's name?" Jonathan demanded.

"Skinsky. He showed us identification. Petrof Skinsky."

They left the port and went back into the center of town. There they asked some of the local people if they had ever heard of Petrof Skinsky.

"I've heard of him, all right," one of them said. "That's the man whose body they found yesterday in the churchyard. His throat had been torn open. Some wild animal must have attacked him." He gave them a dark look. "Or perhaps something else killed him."

Back at their hotel, Van Helsing said, "Something else, indeed. Dracula has escaped us. Now we have no idea where he is. Let's rest now and meet this evening to make a new plan."

That evening they all met in the professor's room to decide on their next step.

"I have been thinking," Mina said. "The Count's castle is a goodly distance from here, up in the mountains. There are only three ways he can get home. He can go by road, by train, or in a boat. I don't think he'll go by road because we could catch up with him too easily. He would never take a chance leaving his box of earth unattended on a train. So he must plan to go by water. He'll travel up the river in a boat."

"You make a good point, Miss Mina," Van Helsing said. "Remember the last time I hypnotized you? You heard the sound of water, but not the same as when the Count was on the ship."

Mina said, "We should ask ourselves, how did the Count leave his castle? Remember that Jonathan told us the gypsies came for him. It would make sense that he has hired some gypsies to take him back. They will carry him up the river Danube to a point near the Borgo Pass. From there it would be an easy trip up to Castle Dracula."

"Once more Miss Mina, your study of the records of this case has paid off," the professor said. "You see, but we are blind. The question is, how can we catch the Count while he is still helpless?"

"I'll buy a steam boat," Arthur said. "I know how to operate one. We'll be able to travel faster than any gypsies."

"And I'll get hold of some horses," Quincey said. "I'll follow the shore of the river in case he lands anywhere along the way."

"I must go with Arthur," Jonathan said. "A steam boat is most likely to catch up with the gypsies first. I insist on having the chance to get revenge on the Count because of what he has done to Mina. I must destroy Dracula."

Dr. Seward said he would ride with Quincey on the horses.

"And I will take Miss Mina by carriage straight up to Castle Dracula," Van Helsing said. "We'll arrive before any of you."

"Not for the world," Jonathan said. "She must stay away from there."

"I understand your concern," the professor said. "But Miss Mina must come with us. If Dracula escapes us this time, it will not matter how far away she is. We need everyone's help. We need to get to his castle and make sure it is no refuge to him."

"He's right, Jonathan," Mina said. "I'm not afraid."

Jonathan didn't like the idea, but he agreed.

They made all their preparations. They took rifles to shoot the wolves they expected to find. Even Mina carried a pistol.

Van Helsing handed out crosses to ward off vampires.

"What about Mina," Jonathan asked. "You didn't give her one."

"I can't take one, dear," Mina said. "You forget that I'm already half vampire myself."

Chapter 19

For three days they moved separately into the wild mountains and mysterious valleys of Transylvania, the most remote part of Romania. Jonathan was impatient as he and Arthur rode the puffing steam boat up the river. He was worried about Mina.

Quincey and Dr. Seward rode their horses along the bank. They led extra horses to have them fresh and so that Jonathan and Arthur might join them if they needed to.

Professor Van Helsing and Mina drove along in the carriage the professor had rented. They were headed as fast as they could go toward the Borgo Pass. They wanted to reach the castle of Count Dracula before he got there himself. When they stopped at an inn, a peasant woman there saw the scar in the shape of a cross on Mina's forehead. The woman drew back in terror. After that, Mina wore the brim of her hat low to hide the mark.

Arthur and Jonathan finally caught up to the gypsies' boat. They could see them ahead, but at that point the river passed over rapids. The gypsies knew how to navigate them with their lighter craft, but Arthur crashed his steamboat into the rocks. Jonathan had to fasten the boat to the shore, while Arthur made repairs as quickly as he could.

Mina and Professor Van Helsing hurried on. The country grew wilder and wilder as they moved into the mountains. Mina had seen nothing like it. No more houses appeared along the road. Everything was desolate.

All day, Mina slept. Van Helsing was not surprised that she was tired. But he became alarmed when he could not waken her. The power that the vampire held over her was growing as they approached his castle. Yet they could not turn back.

Finally, they reached the Borgo Pass. It was a wild, desolate place. Mina pointed to a track leading up the hill to one side.

"This is the way to go, Professor," she said.

"How do you know?"

"Jonathan came this way when he first approached Castle Dracula. He described it exactly in his diary."

Was that it? Van Helsing wondered. Or was the castle drawing Mina onward now? Was she falling completely under Dracula's sway?

The professor became even more worried. Before they reached the remote castle, they stopped and fixed dinner from a basket of food they had purchased in town. Mina would not eat.

"I have no appetite," she said. It was another bad sign.

Finally, they came in sight of Castle Dracula itself. A cold wind blew down from the higher mountains.

"Mina, we must camp here for the night," Van Helsing told her.

He built a fire while Mina made a bed of the furs they had brought. Around it, the professor arranged a circle of garlic flowers.

He stepped over by the fire and said, "Come closer, Miss Mina. Get warm."

She rose, but she did not come closer. "I can't," she said.

"Good. That means the garlic circle will protect us. If you cannot move outside it, the vampires cannot move inside."

The horses made frightened noises and kept pulling at their ropes all night. Van Helsing went several times to calm them. During the darkest part of the night, when it was almost dawn, the fire died down. That was when the first flakes of snow started. Soon snow was swirling all around them.

"Professor, look!" Mina said. She was pointing.

Through the flakes, Van Helsing could make out three figures in white. At first, he wasn't sure what they were. Then he saw they were three women. They were the same that Jonathan had seen at Castle Dracula. They came closer and closer, but they could not come inside the ring of garlic.

They called out in sweet voices to Mina, "Come, sister. Come to us. Come!"

Mina looked at them in terror and did not move.

Van Helsing was glad. It meant she was not yet one of them. As day broke, the figures faded and disappeared.

At the river bank below, the gypsies who were transporting Dracula's box now carried it off the boat and loaded it onto a wagon. They began to climb the long road toward Castle Dracula. Jonathan and Arthur had not caught up with them in time. They left their steamboat behind and borrowed horses to continue on. Dr. Seward and Quincey Morris, riding by a different road, were also on the track.

Van Helsing rose early and left Mina asleep. He made his way toward the dreadful castle. He found the doors open, but he was afraid of being trapped inside. He broke off the hinges with a hammer to make sure this could not happen. He began his search of the castle.

In a distant part of the building, he found a tomb. A heavy coffin lay inside. With a long bar, he worked to pry the lid off. He heard something far off from outside the castle. It was the howl of a wolf. Should he return to Mina? No, he thought, wolves only threaten her life. I must try to save her soul. I cannot leave this work undone.

Inside the coffin was the first of the three women. She was very beautiful. As he gazed on her lovely face, Van Helsing wondered if he would have the nerve to do what he knew had to be done.

He found the second tomb. The woman who lay inside that one was even more beautiful than the first. And the third tomb held the most radiant woman of all of them. Van Helsing's head began to spin.

I will never be able to do it, he thought. It will be too much for me.

Then he noticed the fourth tomb, larger than all the others. On it was carved one word: DRACULA.

This was the home of the king of all vampires. He knew that, for now, it was empty. He put garlic around the entrance so that the Count could not use it again.

Now he began the awful work of driving stakes through the bodies of the three women. With every blow of the hammer, he trembled. Each woman screeched and plunged and twisted under the stake. Her mouth overflowed with blood. Her pointed teeth showed bare. Her eyes pierced him with a cold and wild stare.

But Van Helsing did not lose his nerve. He moved from one coffin to the other. When he finished driving a stake through a woman's body, a look of peace came over each face. He finished the job by cutting off the head of each of the corpses. Instantly, the bodies turned to dust.

The professor hurried out of the castle and back to where Mina was waiting. She was awake now, unharmed.

"Hurry," she said. "Dracula is getting close. I know it. We must go and meet him."

They walked down the steep hill. The awful snowstorm grew worse. It was terribly cold and gray. Behind them, they could barely see Castle Dracula. It was just a menacing outline against the sky.

Mina was already weak. Walking through the snow was too much for her. She needed to rest. Van Helsing found a little cave near the side of the road. From it they could look all the way down the side of the mountain. At the bottom of the valley, they saw the river Danube. It looked like a black snake. Above it, they were able to make out a wagon struggling along the mountainside. Far behind the wagon, two pairs of men on horseback were riding quickly on two different roads.

"Look through the binoculars and tell me what you see," the professor said.

Mina looked at the distant figures. "I see a box on the wagon," she said. "It's like one of those coffins. And the men around it look like gypsies. They are whipping the horses to make them pull faster."

"Does it look like the men on horseback will catch them?"

"No, I don't think so. The gypsies will be here too soon."

"They are anxious to reach the castle before dark," Van Helsing said. "I don't blame them. But they will have to pass here, and we will stop them if we can."

The snow came down more heavily. Mina could see nothing below. When it cleared again, the wagon and those pursuing it were closer.

"I can see Jonathan!" Mina said. "Yes, I'm sure it's him. And Arthur is with him. The ones coming from the other direction are Dr. Seward and Quincey."

"We will have the gypsies surrounded," Van Helsing said. "Get your pistol ready. I hear the wolves closing in, too. Don't hesitate to shoot them if they come close."

They waited. They gypsies struggled up the hill. Suddenly the snow cleared. For a brief instant the sun came out. It was sinking toward the tops of the mountains.

"In a few minutes it will set," the professor warned. "Then Count Dracula will be free to take any form he wants. He will be home. Our chance to destroy him will be lost, maybe forever." He did not add that Mina, too, would be lost.

Just as the gypsies were reaching the spot where Van Helsing and Mina waited, Jonathan, galloping on his horse, caught up with them.

"Halt!" he called. The gypsies did not speak English, but they knew from his tone what he was saying. At the same time, Quincey Morris and Dr. Seward appeared on the other side of the road.

The gypsies did not obey. Their leader gave a command. Ten of his men surrounded the wagon. They urged the horses to go on even faster but the road was steep.

Dr. Seward and Arthur pointed their rifles at the fleeing gypsies. At the same time, Van Helsing and Mina leaped from behind the rock. They each held out a pistol.

The gypsies stopped and prepared for a fight. Their leader pointed, first at the box on the wagon, then at the setting sun. The battle began.

Jonathan from one side and Quincey from the other began to fight their way toward the wagon. They had to reach it before the sun disappeared.

The gypsies would not let them come close. They fought fiercely, waving clubs and flashing knives, shouting. Wolves howled all around.

Jonathan fought with such determination that the gypsies gave way before him. He hit one, then another, knocking them backward.

He reached the wagon and leapt up onto it. Somehow he was able to lift the heavy box and fling it over the side.

Quincey and the others continued to fight with the gypsies. One of their knives reached Quincey. He grabbed his side. Blood spurted through his fingers.

The wound didn't stop him. He fought on. He made it to one end of the big box and pried the lid with his Bowie knife. Jonathan used his own knife to force off the other end. Arthur and Dr. Seward stood guard, forcing the gypsies back.

The cover of the big box fell off. Inside lay Dracula!

He was pale, a white as the snow that covered the ground. His red eyes burned with pure hatred. But he could see that the sun was finally dipping below the mountains. His face showed a look of triumph. He would escape now. He was sure of it.

At that moment, Jonathan's knife sliced down and cut through the Count's throat. At the same instant, Quincey Morris plunged his big Bowie knife into Dracula's chest.

For a moment, a look of deep peace passed over the Count's features. Then his body turned completely to dust.

Seeing this, the gypsies ran for their lives.

Quincey Morris sank to the ground. Blood was still flowing from his wound. Mina ran to him. All the men gathered around.

"Don't grieve, little lady," Quincey said to Mina. "I have my reward. We have ended the curse forever. It is worth dying to see what I see now. Look!"

They all looked to where Quincey pointed with his last strength. The final gleam of the setting sun showed that Mina's forehead was now as pure and white as the snow. She was a vampire no longer. Her soul was finally free.

Silently and with a smile, Quincey died.

The End

AUTHOR'S NOTE

Thanks for reading!
Luke Hayes is a noted author of books for young readers.
He specializes in classic stories that kids can read for themselves,
or that parents and grandparents can read at story time.
Luke lives in New York's Hudson Valley where he likes to fly kites.
You can contact Luke at LukeHayesAuthor@gmail.com.

J. Porter Publishing

JporterPublishing.com

www.ingramcontent.com/pod-product-compliance
Lightning Source LLC
Chambersburg PA
CBHW030643130626
46552CB00002B/988